PUSHKIN PRESS CLASSICS

TROUBLED WATERS

'She depicts, in superb prose, the brilliant innocence of children and the customs of the old part of Tokyo… a pleasure to read'

MIEKO KAWAKAMI

'Subtle, precise and deft, the five stories in Troubled Waters *are full of longing, written with exceptional control, and – in this sensitive and intelligent translation by Bryan Karetnyk – brimming with the richness and intensity of inner lives'*

LUCY CALDWELL

'A remarkable and devastating introduction to the writing of Ichiyo Higuchi. Troubled Waters *evokes the thorniness of desire with world-weary humour and startling clarity. Steeped in extraordinary compassion, yearning, and beauty, these stories illuminate the complex interior lives and precarious fates of women and girls living on the margins'*

SENAA AHMAD

ICHIYO HIGUCHI (1872–1896) was born into a prosperous family whose fortunes declined sharply over the course of her childhood. After the deaths of her father and brother, she moved with her mother and sisters to a poor Tokyo neighbourhood adjacent to the Yoshiwara pleasure district. In an effort to shore up the family finances, Higuchi began publishing her short stories, which quickly earned her a reputation as a major new writer. Over a brief period she wrote some twenty-one stories, thousands of poems and an extensive diary. She died of tuberculosis shortly after the beginning of this brilliant literary career, aged only twenty-four. From 2004 to 2024 her face appeared on Japan's 5,000-yen note.

BRYAN KARETNYK is a British writer and translator. His translations for Pushkin Press include works by Gaito Gazdanov, Irina Odoevtseva, Jun'ichiro Tanizaki and Ryunosuke Akutagawa. He is also the editor of the Penguin Classics anthology *Russian Émigré Short Stories from Bunin to Yanovsky*.

TROUBLED WATERS

ICHIYO HIGUCHI

TRANSLATED FROM THE JAPANESE
BY BRYAN KARETNYK

PUSHKIN PRESS CLASSICS

Pushkin Press
Somerset House, Strand
London WC2R 1LA

'A Snowy Day' was first published as 'Yuki no hi' in 1893
'New Year's Eve' was first published as 'Otsugomori' in 1894
'Growing Pains' was first published as 'Takekurabe' in 1895
'Troubled Waters' was first published as 'Nigorie' in 1895
'This Mortal Coil' was first published as 'Utsusemi' in 1895

First published by Pushkin Press in 2026

ISBN 13: 978-1-80533-272-5

A CIP catalogue record for this title is available from the British Library

The authorised representative in the EEA is eucomply OÜ,
Pärnu mnt. 139b-14, 11317, Tallinn, Estonia,
hello@eucompliancepartner.com, +33757690241

Cover image: *A Study by the Shoji*, 1910 by Herbert Ponting

Designed and typeset by Tetragon, London
Printed and bound in the United Kingdom by Clays Ltd, Elcograf S.p.A.

Pushkin Press is committed to a sustainable future for our business, our readers and our planet. This book is made from paper from forests that support responsible forestry.

www.pushkinpress.com

1 3 5 7 9 8 6 4 2

TROUBLED WATERS

Contents

Introduction

In February 1894, Higuchi Ichiyō was desperate. Aged only twenty-one and poverty-stricken, she visited a celebrated fortune-teller, hoping that he might change her luck. 'I was born in the year of the monkey, on the twenty-fifth day of the third lunar month,'* she told him.

> This is the sixth year since I lost my father, and I find myself tossed upon the raging waves of adversity in this floating world—yesterday to the east, tomorrow to the west. Whereas once I dwelt above the clouds, amid the moonlight, passing my days in refined pursuit of leisure, I find myself now living in squalor, with an ageing mother to support and a younger sister who knows nothing of the world. Until last year, my life seemed like that of any other girl.

Her tale was no exaggeration. She was, in those days, struggling to eke out a living, running a stationery shop with her mother and younger sister in an area known as Ryūsen-ji, a down-at-heel neighbourhood situated behind Tokyo's red-light

---

* That is, by the Gregorian calendar, 2nd May 1872.

district, the Yoshiwara—a precipitous fall from the life she had formerly known.

Born to a humble family in the twilight years of the shogunate, Higuchi Natsuko (as she was born) was the fourth child and second daughter of a man with scholarly inclinations, who as a farmer had come to the capital to seek both fortune and rank. Through astute political manoeuvring and financial positioning, her father, Noriyoshi, managed to have himself adopted into a samurai family in 1867, only for the class to be abolished by the sweeping reforms of the Meiji Restoration, which began in 1868. Enough money remained, however, to send his favourite daughter in 1886 to the Haginoya, a prestigious private school, where she studied classical poetry alongside the daughters of aristocrats and noblemen. Yet the times were changing, and, under the new Meiji administration, the status and wealth of former samurai decreased; unable to keep pace with the rapidly developing economic environment, the girl's father made a series of imprudent investments, which, by the time of his death from tuberculosis in 1889, hastened by his grief over the death of his eldest son two years previously, ended up ruining the Higuchi family and lumbering his beloved daughter with the burden of financial responsibility. And so, hounded by creditors and distressed by mounting debts, the remaining family had to leave their formerly genteel surroundings for the gritty, unsentimental shadows of the Yoshiwara.

Despite all this, and despite having been jilted by her fiancé shortly after her father's demise, the young woman remained undeterred in her ambitions. Through her education and her father's encouragement, she had nurtured a vocation for literature and was determined to make a career for herself in the *bundan*, Japan's literary elite, not least after having seen the success of her former classmate Miyake Kaho, whose novel *Warbler in the Grove* (1888) had won widespread acclaim, to say nothing of substantial royalties for its author. Determined now to leave her mark on the literary establishment and resolved to support her family through her writing, she adopted the literary pseudonym Ichiyō and, with the help of her mentor (and sometime object of her unrequited affections), Nakarai Tōsui, made her debut with a short story entitled 'Flowers at Dusk' in 1892. Even so, the path to literary acknowledgement would not run straight. Ichiyō's was a tale of perseverance—through poverty and financial struggle, through personal ill health, and through the professional and social limitations that were imposed on her by virtue of her womanhood in male-dominated Meiji Japan.

The advice Ichiyō received that day from the fortune-teller was, ironically, predictable: Resign yourself to the will of Heaven. Yet what Heaven had ordained for Ichiyō was as tragic as it was perhaps heroic. As Ichiyō lamented her lot, she observed: 'I wish I had spent this fleeting life as the moon, shining brightly before it wanes, or as a cherry tree, in blossom for its short season.' How prophetic those words were, for a mere two years later she would be dead from the same disease that had taken her father and brother before her. And yet, by that same stroke, she would also leave behind her a monumental body of work that encompassed some four thousand poems, an extensive diary that so many critics have likened to a novel in itself, a scattering of essays and, crucially, twenty-one short stories, which, bridging as they do the classical and the modern, were pivotal in the development of modern Japanese literature. Truly, her example was the epitome of fleeting genius.

Brief though Ichiyō's life was, her perseverance and dedication to literary art was consummate. Within the short window of her career, her style underwent several major shifts as her writing matured rapidly, and the five stories collected here have been chosen accordingly, not only to present some of her finest writing, but also to showcase each of these stages at its apex.

'A Snowy Day' (1893), which opens this collection, is a gem of Ichiyō's early work. This brief, impressionistic tale of infatuation and the folly of youth is vested in all manner of classical allusions and rich, multilayered poetic imagery and symbolism—all hallmarks of Ichiyō's rococo early style. As a vista of a snow-clad landscape brings the young pseudo-autobiographical narrator to reflect on the past awakening of her maidenly desire, she is ultimately forced to confront her own disenchantment as well as the sorrows and regrets to which her passions have led her. Here, against the intimate interiority of this elegant narrative, untamed urges clash with Confucian ideals of filial piety and Buddhist undertones of the suffering caused by worldly attachments.

'New Year's Eve' (1894), while continuing several of Ichiyō's thematic preoccupations, marks a significant departure, trading as it does the florid ornamentation of her earlier works for a more restrained and direct form of expression. Poetic gesture gives way, likewise, to realism and plot in this account, which sets a young woman's moral dilemma against the bustle of preparations for the New Year. Widely held to be Ichiyō's first masterpiece, this story develops the psychological strain of the author's writing, although the motivation is no longer the emotional vagaries of so much classical poetry, but rather the cold, hard moral ambiguities brought about by penury and social inequality. Borrowing now from the earthy and often ribald urban narratives of Edo-period writers such as Ihara Saikaku (1642–93), Ichiyō takes as her subjects Meiji society's humiliated and insulted—counter to much of the literature of the day—imbuing them with pathos and dignity, and also gentle humour.

It was with 'Growing Pains' (1895), however, that Ichiyō reached the zenith of her artistic maturity. In this, her longest and in many regards most sophisticated piece, she draws bountifully on her own observations of the Yoshiwara and its environs to craft a remarkable coming-of-age tale that has at its core a group of adolescents transitioning—reluctantly—into adulthood. Here, the deftness and poise of Ichiyō's brush conjures forth the life of the licensed quarter, along with its rites and rituals, its great hopes and little tragedies.

Focusing not on the ink-stale subjects of the Yoshiwara's famed geisha and courtesans, but rather on the children in the margins of the quarter, both geographical and social, she subverts all notions of childhood as a time of carefree innocence and, with profound sympathy, presents the loss of what innocence they have not as a necessary step towards their own self-fulfilment, but as the inevitable process of resignation, to everything to which fate and society assign them. Rich in detail, replete with wordplay, it is a nigh-perfect synthesis of Ichiyō's classical training and ambitions as a modern writer.

The melancholy title story of this collection, 'Troubled Waters' (1895), represents a continuation of Ichiyō at the peak of her artistry, but here we encounter the author's work in what is perhaps a darker, more tragic light. While this tale of an unhappy love triangle, involving a courtesan and set in an unnamed pleasure quarter, harks back to beloved themes of so many pieces composed for the kabuki stage and the *bunraku* puppet theatres of the eighteenth century, it removes them from the stricter moral and religious codes of those earlier dramas and replaces their mannered conventionalism with deep and idiosyncratic realism. Eschewing the temptations of melodrama, Ichiyō's by-now-characteristic subtle restraint here reaches a new intensity as she dwells on the hesitations, silences and half-expressed longings of her characters. The result is a narrative in which sympathy and futility intertwine, and in which, as the title of the piece hints, emotional, moral and, ultimately, fatal ambiguities abound.

In the brief yet devastating final piece of this collection, translated here into English for the first time, 'This Mortal Coil' (1895), Ichiyō restates the love-triangle plot, but now in a more rarefied setting and with the level of ambiguity pushed to its limits. Here, the real account of a young woman's descent into torturous mental illness is left scarcely articulated, to be read, as it were, between the lines of once again dream-like prose, which, but for its implicit indictment of middle-class propriety, seems almost to recapture something of the delicate, fleeting quality of Ichiyō's early work, modulated now to express the fragility of life itself.

Translating these works has been both a privilege and a passion. Each of Ichiyō's narratives is written predominantly, if not entirely, in classical Japanese: that is, a strictly literary form of the written language that even in the Meiji era had maintained, unlike the vernacular Japanese spoken in Ichiyō's day, all the inflections and conventions handed down from the Heian period across a millennium. To draw a more meaningful comparison for readers less familiar with Japanese, it is, with all the necessary provisos, as though the writers of the late-Victorian era still wrote in the English of Chaucer. Even so, Ichiyō's prose, from beginning to last, stands out among that of her peers for its heavy debt to classical poetry and technique, so replete is it with the rhythms and cadence of traditional Japanese verse, to say nothing of its profusion of poetic allusions and extensive use of punning. It is also written with classical punctuation, whereby a paragraph or even an entire story might be written across the duration of a single period, the narration mingling with character voices that intrude unannounced. It is for this reason, and in the hope that the reader might have a more proximate experience of reading Ichiyō, that I have preserved her own idiosyncratic paragraphing and dispensed with quotation marks.

Even at the outset of her literary career, Ichiyō wondered about posterity. 'As someone who has taken up the brush, I cannot allow myself to produce work that will be thrown away after a single reading,' she wrote of her literary apprehensions as early as 1891,

> Human nature may be fickle. And though ours is a world in which what today brings joy may tomorrow be discarded, yet if I make my appeal to true emotions and depict that truth faithfully, then will Ichiyō's scribblings not have some worth? It is not that I desire splendid apparel or stately mansions. But for the sake of one fleeting moment, I do not wish to tarnish a name that may last a thousand years. [...] Even so, if all this ink and paper be spent in vain, I shall look upon it as the will of Heaven.

It may have been the will of Heaven that Ichiyō died soon after that desperate visit to the fortune-teller, but time has proved that her efforts were far from having been in vain. Ichiyō has gone down in history as Japan's first woman writer to earn a living from her writing, and her legacy, which redefined Japanese literature for the modern age, lives on today. Her life and works are adapted for stage and screen, and her diaries have been serialized on radio. Many of Japan's leading writers, including Enchi Fumiko, Tawada Yōko, Itō Hiromi and Kakuta Mitsuyo, have produced translations of her works into modern Japanese, while others such as Kawakami Mieko have gone so far as to claim Ichiyō as their greatest influence. Those thousand years may still be a way off, but one thing is certain: Ichiyō has already more than vindicated herself, appealing to the deepest and most humane of people's emotions, depicting unflinchingly what lies true in their hearts.

B.S.K.

A SNOWY DAY

(Yuki no hi)

AS SNOWFLAKES FLUTTER gently in the air like the dancing wings of butterflies, dusting the earth as far as the eye can see in a powder of argent, their six-petalled crystals land on trees stripped bare by winter, a vista of spring blossoms to come. How I envy those whom such a scene moves to compose verse and song enumerating the snow's many beauties alongside those of the moon and flowers. Alas! for me the endlessly falling snow conjures but sorrowful and bitter memories of a past that cannot be shaken off. Myriad regrets I have, and each one of them in vain. What a waste—what impiety!—to have forsaken the land of my ancestors, to have disobeyed even the aunt who raised me with such tenderness. Now I have besmirched the very name my parents bestowed on me. They called me Tama—their Pearl—believing the word impervious to tarnish. Never would they have dreamt that my wretched existence would end up as worthless as a broken tile. Yet into a mountain stream I fell, and, borne by the current, I found myself in troubled waters. My youth was my downfall, my sin love, and the go-between a snowy day.

I was born in the mountains, in a hamlet where the grass grows deep. Ours was an eminent family, whose name, Usui, was known throughout the region. An only child, I was the last in the family line. Both my parents departed this world, alas, before their time, and so it was my aunt—who had married into another family, only then to lose her husband—who returned home to take charge of me. And yet, from the time that I was almost three, she devoted herself to my upbringing as though I were her own. Even the gentle, tender love of a parent, dare I say, could not have surpassed hers. When I reached my seventh year, she arranged for a master of calligraphy to tutor me, and herself spared no efforts instructing me in music. But even so, no gatekeeper can check the passage of years… One day, the tucked waist of my maiden's kimono was let down, and I began to pluck my eyebrows. What a joy it was to wrap a woman's broad *obi* about my waist. And yet, to think back on it now—what folly! I may have grown as tall as my years decreed, but there could be no comparing my cultivation to that of the young ladies of the capital. In that respect, I was a mere child, quite unaware of the differences between men and women. My life was in all regards unclouded, sans care or worry. Then came the winter of my fifteenth year. How could anyone have known the love that was in my heart—a love that was unknown then even to me? Still, driving winds carried with them rumours that reached my dear aunt's ears. Those rumours held that I was in love.

The world in which we live is one of error and mistake. Rumours break like waves in some nameless river, dappling our sleeves with falsehood. The reason for those torrents, for those tears, was Katsuragi Ichirō, a teacher at the school I attended. He was a native of Tokyo. A fine figure of a man, he was well liked by the pupils because he was kind of heart, and the merest mention of his name provoked admiration in all. He lodged half a mile from me, to the north, in a little hut on the grounds of the Hōshō-ji temple. I had been his pet ever since I first set foot in the school. But ah! how true is the saying that old habits die hard. Sometimes he would pay me a visit, and on other occasions I would accompany him home. The stories he would tell me were filled with many a stimulating lesson. He would treat me just like a little sister, which of course delighted me, having no siblings of my own. At school, I even took a certain pride in all this, but to think back on it now, it must have struck others as very odd indeed. For although our relations were as pure as the driven snow, I was no longer a child and had begun to wear my hair up in the *shimada* style thought suitable for young women. And besides, this man was now in his early thirties. Ah! what folly it was to ignore those learned books, where it is written that boys and girls should be separated after their seventh year...*

The wildfires of rumour, once lit, are nigh impossible to extinguish. Believing our conduct improper, the villagers began to make insinuations. Alas! that my precious pearl should be tarnished so, my aunt lamented. What will it bring but a lifetime of misery and disappointment? Mark

* Neo-Confucian manuals published in the Edo period, many principles of which persisted in Higuchi's day, advocated for the strict separation of the sexes at this age.

my words. Have you forgotten the troubles I took in rearing you? To think that the last girl in the Usui line would behave with such depravity! Do you know what people are saying? She'd never have turned out that way if her parents were alive! It's your poor mother that I feel sorry for, she who on her deathbed begged me to take care of you. She was so weak that she could scarcely speak! Oh, this is more than I can bear! Whoever wrote that a parent must grope their way in the dark—how well he knew that of which he wrote! To think that everything has been in vain, after all I've done for you. We'll wind up the laughing-stock of the village! Frankly, I haven't the least idea what to do now—neither for the sake of my dearly departed sister, nor for the good name of the Usui family! A woman of few words ordinarily, my aunt now carried on admonishing me most emphatically, although in hushed tones, for fear that the neighbours might overhear. At first, I was utterly bewildered, insensible to her words, but then she spoke more pointedly. Now listen here, Tama! It's clear that Katsuragi loves you, and that you in turn pine for him. Be that as it may, there are rules to be observed in such matters. We Usui have never married outside this village, let alone anyone from the capital. A fine scholar though Katsuragi may be, we know nothing of him or of his background. It's unthinkable that he could ever be allowed to join a family of such pedigree as ours. No matter how much you may love him, marriage is out of the question. And if these are just rumours, which I hope they are, then so much the better. You are not to see him again, do you hear? Henceforth, you shall give him a wide berth. You won't be needing lessons from him any more. That I have treated that man with any respect at all until now is only out of love for you. To bow and scrape before this worthless outsider is beneath me. All these years, I have raised you to the best of my abilities. People always said what a lovely girl you were. And how proud you made me too! Only for him to come and envelop you in a miasma of scandal… But there's nothing for it now. What's done is done. Now you must repair the damage you've caused, clear your name, and set my mind at ease. At any rate, that man is your enemy, and if you have any thought for me or your family's reputation, you will put this Katsuragi Ichirō out of your mind—lock, stock and barrel. You are never to see him again, do you hear? Even if you should happen to pass by his lodgings. These directives, piled one on top of another, tore so cruelly at my heart that I could hold back my tears no longer. Ah! how I wept and wept, my face buried in my sleeves.

What injustice this is! Let the whole village gossip and shun me! What do I care? But for my own aunt, who raised me, to doubt my innocence and accuse me of sullying myself like this?! It isn't as if I met Mr Katsuragi only yesterday, either. Our conduct has been quite proper. You ought to see that. It's heartless that you should let yourself be swayed by idle gossip! Would that I could cut open my heart to prove my innocence! Thus did I protest. But whatever emotions may have lurked at the bottom of my heart were like wild horses whose reins I could not hold.

Even a solitary bamboo shutter drawn between friends may cause heartache. Across the half mile that separated us, the stern gaze of the villagers was an impediment to our meeting. Soon, the cold winds of winter began to blow, stripping the trees bare. How I envied the scattering red maple leaves that would be borne towards him. I would gaze off into the distance to see where they would go, and the sight of the forest beckoned to me. Recollections of that hut where he lived, on the edge of the village, came back to me. The evening tolling of the bell at the Hōshō-ji temple echoed plaintively. While my spirit was drawn towards the heavens, yet my aunt's admonitions weighed me down. I did not even dare so much as to turn in his direction, and so I waited and waited for the day when he would come to me. But the rumours had spread, and doubtless this gave him pause. I received no word from him. As our separation continued, I seemed to live a thousand autumns. The New Year eventually came, bringing with it fresh hopes and prayers and celebrations. On the seventh day, my aunt betook herself to a neighbouring village to pay her respects to some relatives there. The sky, which had been cloudy since the morning, was growing darker and darker. Although the winds had died down, yet the bitter cold cut to the bone. I felt terribly alone. Then, all of a sudden, I spotted a flurry of snow from the heavens. Won't Auntie be cold? I mused by the warmth of the brazier. The snow was getting heavier: unrelenting, it now fell like cotton. Soon it had blanketed everything, the garden, the fence… I opened the low window ever so slightly.

The fields and farmlands behind the house, as far as the eye could see, were obscured entirely. The forest where he lived, the one on which I gazed out daily, was now the same colour as the sky. What was he doing now? I wondered, my feelings in disarray.

If there is a god of misfortune, then he had certainly set his sights on me. What can I have been thinking? In that moment, I knew neither good nor evil. Driven by a sense of longing, I fled my family home, showing a complete disregard for all and sundry.

It did not occur to me then that this was the end, that never again would I look back on those eaves that were so dear to me. In my impatience, I went hurrying out of the gate. Miss! Wherever are you off to in all this snow? And without an umbrella, too! The voice that had so startled me belonged to our farmhand, Heisuke, a loyal but rather slow-witted man. I'm going to meet Auntie! I lied. Oh, but surely she'll spend the night there, given the weather and all? But if you really want someone to go and meet her, Miss, I'll go, and you can wait here. I wouldn't dream of it! And besides, she'll be so proud to see me make my way in the snow, all by myself. You just stay here and pretend you never saw me. Well, I think you're mad, said Heisuke, wearing a louche, broad grin, but if your mind's made up, you'd better take this. He handed me the umbrella. Just mind how you go now, lest you slip and fall! Wherever there is a bond between two souls, their longing will colour everything, I thought to myself, recalling lines from a certain poem. That my aunt had been so cold, so strict with me had, of course, been for my own benefit; but only later did I come to appreciate just how undeserving of her efforts I had been.

I was in love with my teacher, to be sure, but despite this I had never imagined, not even in my dreams, that I should one day call that man my husband, or that we should elope together. The two of us drifted aimlessly. Like the black bamboo by my window, bent by the heavy snows, we were broken by the burden of our sins. To quit the home of my ancestors, forsaking my aunt: such was my dream, my wicked desire that snowy day.

The resentment I now feel for my husband is in vain. Splendid indeed are the flowers of the capital, but how could a mountain tree such as myself ever have hoped to rival them? I am forsaken and alone, withered like grass in winter. Sometimes, with teardrops on my sleeves, I question the past and realize that it was all a mistake. Later, winds brought with them news from my village: my departure had plunged my aunt into such terrible grief that she expired in the autumn of that same year. But it is too late for regrets now. I have nothing left in this fleeting world. In protecting the honour of a man who is indifferent to me, I have tried to carry a strange and unfamiliar tune. How right Shikibu* was when she wrote that the first snow falls on a world of ever-mounting sorrows. Now here it is again this year, unaware of

* Murasaki Shikibu (*c.*978–*c.*1031), the poet and noblewoman best known as the author of *The Tale of Genji*.

the torments it brings, sparing with its white veil the blushes of a broken fence, while boasting of its own splendour, as though to say, Behold this, my work!… I loved it, too—once upon a time.

NEW YEAR'S EVE

(Ōtsugomori)

I.

NOT ONLY DID the well have a pulley with a rope more than twenty fathoms long, but the kitchen faced north, and the chill hibernal winds would go whistling right through it. Lamenting how unbearable all this was, O-Mine would steal moments in front of the stove, prodding at the fire to keep warm, but, just as saplings grow into great trees, these moments, too, turned into long hours ere long, and she would be given a stern talking-to. The old woman from the agency who introduced her there had said that there were six children all told, but that only the eldest and the youngest were usually to be found at home. She had also mentioned that the mistress could be a little temperamental, but, provided that O-Mine knew how to conceal her emotions, there was nothing to worry about—in other words, the lady of the house was easily flattered, and so she would be as accommodating as the girl's conduct merited. Theirs was the richest family in the neighbourhood, and also the most penny-pinching; fortunately, however, the master was a soft touch, and so there was every chance that O-Mine might yet be given a little extra pocket money. If you don't like it there, just send word, the woman from the agency had told her. A word, mind—you needn't bother with any long-winded explanations. I'll be glad to find you a position somewhere else. Besides, if you want my advice, the secret to getting on in service is duplicity. Well! thought the girl. What an awful thing to say! But then, everything is a matter of perspective. And at any rate, O-Mine did not want to be beholden to this woman, so she decided that if only she applied herself and worked diligently, her new employer would be sure to take to her—and that is how she came to serve such a devil of a family. On the third day after her trial period ended, the young seven-year-old mistress was due to attend a dance rehearsal in the afternoon. The morning was a frosty one. Come on! Come on! the mistress cried out at the crack of dawn, her voice more startling than an alarm clock. Banging the bamboo ashtray from the warmth of her bed, she shouted that things had to be got ready, hot water had to be prepared for the child's morning bath, and the child herself given a proper scrubbing. In the blink of an eye, O-Mine had her obi tied and her sleeves tucked up. When she went out to the well, the moonlight was still reflected in the washbasin, and the cold wind that stung her skin blew away all her lingering dreaminess. The bath may have been deep, but it was not big; yet to fill it up O-Mine had to fill her two pails thirteen times over from the well, dripping with perspiration as she carried them, in spite of the bitter cold. The straps on the old pair of *geta* she wore for wet work had come loose, and they were impossible to wear unless she clenched her toes. All this, combined with the heavy loads she had to carry, made her unsteady on her feet; she slipped on the ice around the washbasin and fell flat on her side, hitting her shin so hard against the side of the well that her pale skin, which rivalled the very snow in whiteness, turned a vivid shade of violet almost instantly. To make matters worse, she had upset the pails as she fell, and, although one lay still intact, the other was broken beyond repair. O-Mine had no idea how much the pail had cost, but, to see the veins bulging on the mistress's forehead, you would have thought she had lost the woman a small fortune. The mistress just kept glaring at the girl all throughout breakfast while she waited on her. Not a word about it was said that day, but afterwards O-Mine was lectured day and night that things in this house cost money and must not be taken for granted, and she was informed that she would be punished if she treated things without due care simply because they were not her own. On top of all that, whenever there were visitors, the mistress would tell them all about the accident, which was terribly humiliating for poor O-Mine. From then on, she had to take great care in everything she did, lest there be another mishap. There are many families in this world that employ maids to keep house, but doubtless none that had quite the turnover the Yamamuras did. It was nothing for them to go through two a month; and if some girls ran away after only three or four days, there were others who fled even after a single night. Ask the mistress how many maids had served the family since the dawn of time, and her sleeves would have been left threadbare from trying to count them all up.* O-Mine, however, had both perseverance and forbearance, and, if ever they were cruel to her, she would humbly endure it as the will of Heaven. And besides, not in all of Tokyo, vast city though it was, could any other girl be found who wanted to work as a maid for the Yamamura family. And so O-Mine was to be praised for her dedication and fine work ethic—and, as the menfolk were quick to point out, it didn't hurt that she was a flawless beauty, too.

O-Mine received word that her only uncle had been taken ill that autumn, shortly after which he had been forced to close his grocer's shop and move to cheaper lodgings in one of the neighbourhood's back alleys. Her fastidious employer paid her wages in advance, which was tantamount to having sold herself into slavery, and so, much as she might have wanted it, she didn't dare ask to be allowed to go and visit him. What's more, whenever the mistress sent O-Mine out on errands, she all but timed her trips down to the minute, and, although she might have considered sneaking out, rumours travelled fast, and then all her hard work and forbearance would have been for naught. Worse still, if she lost her job, it would be a burden on her poor uncle, and the very notion of troubling a man who was barely scraping by from one day to the next seemed unconscionable. Alas, with no prospect of leaving the Yamamura household, letters would have to suffice for the time being.

---

* The reference is to the practice of counting out large numbers by using the warp or weft of the fabric in one's sleeve.

The last month of the year is wont to put everybody in a fluster. How the girls of the Yamamura household fretted over their choice of clothes, determined as they were to get dressed up in their finery, and all because they had heard that an exciting new play had had its opening night only the day before yesterday. Not wanting to miss it, they made such a fuss, and, surprisingly enough, the entire household was invited to see it on the fifteenth of the month. Ordinarily, O-Mine would have been delighted to accompany the family to the theatre, but with her parents dead and her only living relative confined to the sickbed, it seemed improper to enjoy an entertainment. Not wanting to offend her employers, she asked whether she might be allowed to visit her uncle instead of going to the theatre. Because of her recent good conduct, she was told that if she left early and came back in good time, she could go the next day. Scarcely had O-Mine remembered to offer her humblest thanks than she found herself in a rickshaw, wondering when, oh when, would she at last arrive in Koishikawa.

Her uncle lived in the Hatsune-chō district. The name, literally meaning First Song, may conjure up the joyous sounds of spring, yet it in fact belonged to an impoverished area, where only the bush warbler's haunting cries echoed. Her uncle—Honest Yasubei, they called him—was a local fixture and had sold aubergines and radishes from Tamachi to Kikuzaka, his shiny bald pate, like a copper kettle, a veritable beacon to customers. And they do say, after all, that the gods of fortune dwell within the heads of the honest! His was the sort of business that required scant capital, and he sold only cheap items in bulk. He had none of those first pick of the season delicacies: there were no baby cucumbers packed into little boat-shaped containers or matsutake mushrooms bundled up like straw. People laughed that he laid in only those vegetables that were cheap and bountiful; but even so, his regulars were loyal, and somehow he had been able to eke out a living, providing for his wife and son. When his little boy, Sannosuke, turned eight, he had even been able to send him to a school for the poor, where the tuition cost five *rin* per month. But then it happened. The autumn that year was cold, and one morning towards the end of the ninth month, a chill wind cut right through him. Then later, as he was carrying back to his house the produce that he had just bought at the market in Kanda, he came down with a fever and a bout of rheumatism. Three months had passed since that day. Unable to work, he had been forced to make cutbacks at home, where they ate less and less with each passing day; eventually, he had no choice but to sell his scales and fold up the business. He and his family then left the shop on the high street and moved to a dwelling in one of the back alleys, where he paid a rent of only fifty *sen* per month. He went with the intention of moving back someday, but at least there they would not have to worry about feeling shamefaced in front of the neighbours. What a pitiful figure he cut, the sick man alone in the rickshaw, beetling off to some dark corner of the neighbourhood, his scant belongings, such as they were, clutched in a single hand... As she stepped down from her own rickshaw, O-Mine asked herself where her uncle and his family might be. She peered over at a confectioner's shop with kites and paper balloons hanging from the eaves, wondering whether she might chance to see Sannosuke among the group of boys crowding at the door. Disappointed not to spot him there, she gazed absentmindedly at the passers-by. There, on the opposite side of the street, she saw a scrawny boy carrying a bottle of medicine; he looked too tall and too thin to be Sannosuke, but still there was an uncanny resemblance in the face. When she hurried over to get a closer look, she was met with the words, Hello, O-Mine! So, it *is* you, Sannosuke? Now there's a stroke of luck! They set off together, past the sake shop, past the sweet-potato vendor, deeper and deeper into the back streets. When at last they came to an alley where the gutter boards covering the muddy ditches rattled, Sannosuke ran on ahead and, as he reached the door of a certain house, called out, Pa! Ma! I've brought O-Mine back with me!

What?! Our O-Mine's come back to us, has she? said Yasubei, sitting up in bed. His wife set down the sewing that she took in to earn a bit of extra money and, delighted, took the girl's hand, saying, Well now, this *is* a surprise! O-Mine looked around. The room was small—only six *tatami* mats in size—and had only a single cupboard. Of course, a house like this had no need of cabinets or chests of drawers. There was no sight of the oblong brazier they had once owned, either; instead, there was just a cheap-looking Imado-ware square box, which appeared to be the only item of furniture they had. Indeed, it was so spartan that there was no sign of even a rice chest. How sad, thought O-Mine, taking all this in, that there should be people still enjoying the theatre on a day like today. It was enough to bring tears to her eyes. That's quite a draught coming in. You should be wrapped up in bed, Uncle! she said, pulling the blanket, which was as hard and stiff as a rice cracker, over the old man's shoulders. You must have endured a lot of hardship. You look as though you've lost weight, too, Auntie. You mustn't worry so much, otherwise you'll make yourself ill. And besides, you're getting better and better each day, aren't you, Uncle? That's what your letters said, so I had to come and see for myself—I was just waiting for the day when I could get some time off at long last. What? Not at all, the house is just fine. The important thing is that you get well again as soon as possible. That way, you can move back into the high street and reopen the shop. I did want to bring you a present, Uncle, but it's such a long way, and I was impatient to get here. I came as quick as I could, but the rickshaw driver's legs seemed to be going ever so slowly, and I missed the sweet shop. It's not much, but, here, please take what little I have left of the pocket money the Yamamuras gave me. You see, when some of their relatives came to visit from Kōji-machi, the elderly mistress was in pain because of a stomach ailment, so I spent all night massaging her back, and the next day she gave me this and told me to buy myself an apron. What can I say? My employers are a hard lot, but there are others who've been good to me. So, please, Uncle, I'd be glad if you'd take the money.

It's not as though I had to slave away for it. Oh, and I was also given this drawstring purse and this collar for an under-kimono. The collar's only plain, but won't you have it, Auntie? And if you altered the purse a little, it would be perfect for Sannosuke to carry his bento box in. You are still attending school, aren't you, Sannosuke? Oh, do show me your copy book! On and on she went… Her own father had died when she was seven years old. He had been commissioned to build a storehouse, and, as he climbed the scaffolding, trowel in hand, to give it a second coat, he turned to say something to one of the other men down below and—for all his many years of experience, it must have been a black-star day in the almanac, perhaps even the anniversary of the Buddha's death—went toppling over and fell all the way to the ground. The paving had been dug up so that the work could take place, and so he cracked his head open on a pile of masonry. There was nothing that could be done for him. He was forty-one and fast approaching the most inauspicious year of a man's life: it is little wonder that people dread it so.* Her mother, Yasubei's sister, had come to live with him after her husband's death, but two years later she, too, had died unexpectedly after falling ill with influenza. Thereafter, Yasubei and his wife had been like parents to the girl. Now in her eighteenth year, she felt an inexpressible debt of gratitude to

---

* Known in Japan as *yakudoshi*, or 'years of calamity', the forty-second year is traditionally believed to be among the most inauspicious in a man's life.

them. Sannosuke called her sister, and she loved him like a brother. Come over here, she said to him, and patted him on the back as she looked at him. It must be hard for you, all alone, with your father ill as he is. And with New Year just around the corner, too. Why don't I buy you something to cheer you up? After all, we can't have you being a bother to your mother at a time like this. A bother to her? O-Mine's uncle retorted. He may be all of eight years old, but he's a grown boy, big and strong. Ever since I've been confined to this bed, I've been unable to work and earn money, while our debts just go on piling up. The boy didn't want to stand idly by, seeing that we were in such dire straits, so now he goes out with that lad from the salted-fish shop in the high street, hawking freshwater clams. For every eight *sens*' worth he sells, Sannosuke is bound to sell ten! Surely, the gods of heaven and earth can see what filial piety that boy has?! At any rate, it's the boy who's paying for my medicine, so you ought to be singing his praises, O-Mine! he cried, pulling the blanket over his head as his voice choked with tears. He adores school and never causes us any trouble, either, her aunt added. He just eats his breakfast and goes skipping out that door, then he comes straight home at three without stopping to play. I don't mean to crow, but you should hear how his teacher praises him! Oh, it breaks my heart to send the boy out selling clams in this cold weather with only straw sandals on his little feet—and all because we're so poor. Tears dampened her aunt's cheeks, too. O-Mine hugged Sannosuke close and said, Well, well, was there ever a boy as good to his parents as you?

Big and strong you may be—but still, you're only seven. Doesn't it hurt your shoulders, carrying that pole across them when you go hawking? Don't the straw sandals cut your feet? If you wait just a little longer, I'll come home and help you take care of Uncle. How could I have felt so sorry for myself only this morning, complaining about the ice-cold rope and the well, when my young cousin, who should be studying, is out hawking clams? Oh, it's high time I grew up! Uncle, please let me quit my job. I'll leave service and come home as soon as possible, she said, breaking down in tears. Moved by this, Sannosuke looked down at the ground, lest she see his tears. As he did so, O-Mine spotted a hole at the seam of the shoulder of the robes he was wearing, right where the pole he carried would rest; it was painful for her to see. No sooner had O-Mine suggested quitting her job than Yasubei dubbed the very idea unthinkable. I know you mean well, he said, but what would you do when you came back? As a woman, you'd scarcely be able to earn a thing here. And besides, the Yamamuras have already paid your wages in advance. No, it's out of the question! A first job is always vital. You mustn't let them think that you had to go home because you couldn't take it. Go and work hard for Mr Yamamura. I won't be ill for much longer. Once I'm a little better, I'll be ready to get back to work. In another few weeks, the year will be out, and the new year and spring will be here, bringing with them better fortune. Patience and perseverance in everything—that should be your motto. Yours too, Sannosuke, he said, his tears now subdued. It seems a pity not to be able to offer you more—after all, it isn't every day that we see you—but we do have some of those *imagawa* red-bean cakes and taro broth that you like. You can have as much of those as you please! he said, these words of hospitality cheering him. But his gratification was short-lived. I don't like to be a burden, he continued, but, with New Year's just around the corner, these hardships weigh heavily on me. And no, I don't just mean this illness. You see, when I first took ill, I borrowed ten yen on a three-month term from a moneylender in Tamachi. He took one and a half yen in interest, leaving me with eight yen and fifty *sen*. I borrowed the money back at the end of the ninth lunar month, so the repayment is almost due. What am I to do? Your aunt and I have been trying so hard to think of a solution. Her fingers are worked to the bone with all the piecework she does, but she scarcely makes even ten *sen* a day doing that. And we can hardly ask Sannosuke to do more than he's already doing… But the man you work for, O-Mine, well, he must own at least a hundred tenement houses in Shirokane! Even though he rents them out for very little money, there are so many of them that he's able to live in the lap of luxury. I once had a spot of business near where you work, O-Mine; I got as far as the gate and saw the storehouse they were building. Why, it must have cost more than a thousand *ryō*! Now there's a man of means! And if you've been working for him for a year, and if he's taken to you—well, then he might not be averse to helping you out a little bit, mightn't he? If at the end of the month I were to throw myself at the moneylender's mercy and beg him to rewrite the terms of the loan, all I'd need to pay is another term of interest and I'd gain another three months to pay in full. This may sound like greed on my part, but what kind of parents would we be if we can't even buy some mochi from the shop on the high street and offer the boy some *zōni*, as is customary, for the first three days of the new year? All I'd need is two yen by the end of the month. I hate to ask, but do you think you might ask your employer for it? O-Mine reflected for a moment before saying, Very well, Uncle. I'll do just that. Difficult as things are, I'll ask for an advance on my wages. The Yamamuras' wealth isn't quite what it might seem, but, seeing as the sum is so small, and given how much it would help, I'll explain things as best I can. I doubt they'll refuse me. In any case, I'll do what I can for you. Now I'd best be off. It'll be spring when I see you next*—I hope we'll be all smiles by then, she said. I'll send the money somehow. Or why not have Sannosuke come and fetch it for you? Yes, that would be better. I'd bring it myself, but, what with the festivities, I doubt I'll have a moment to spare. I do feel bad asking him to come such a long way, but don't worry, I'll look after him. I'll make sure to have everything squared away by noon on New Year's Eve. Having given her word, O-Mine set off back to the Yamamura residence.

* In Higuchi's day, the lunar calendar was still in effect, hence New Year falling in spring.

2.

Ishinosuke, the eldest of the Yamamura children, had a different mother from his younger siblings, and, to make matters worse, his father's love for him was slight. Ten years ago, he had learnt of the old man's intention to have Ishinosuke adopted and to name the boy's younger sister as his heir. The whole affair was no laughing matter, but while in the past disinheritance might have been a distinct possibility, there was no way that he could be disowned under the new laws. And so now the boy did just as he pleased, causing his stepmother no end of grief and disregarding his father entirely. When he turned fifteen, he began to act with recklessness. For all that his complexion was dark, he had rugged good looks and intelligent eyes, so it was little wonder that the daughters of the neighbourhood were rumoured to be sweet on him. However, his wildest exploits he saved for the licensed quarter in Shinagawa. He loved nothing more than to go tearing around in a rickshaw in the dead of night, waking up every delinquent in the area to go carousing with him, and, whenever they would cry out for more drink and snacks, he would empty his wallet with abandon. To leave the family fortune to him would be like taking a lighted match to the oil in the storehouse, his stepmother was forever lamenting to his father. The whole fortune will go up in smoke, leaving us to stand amid the ashes! And then what will we do? It's his brothers I feel sorry for. And yet, I doubt there's a soul alive who would adopt this prodigal wretch. Having discussed the matter among themselves, they resolved to set aside a certain sum of money and set the boy up early as head of a cadet branch of the family, but young Ishinosuke refused to be taken in by their machinations and blithely paid them no mind. Firstly, I shall require a settlement of 10,000 yen, plus a monthly stipend, he said. Furthermore, you will not stop me frequenting the pleasure district. And when Father dies, I'll be the one to take over as head of the family. My word shall be law, and I shall be accorded all due deference. If they want to offer so much as a single stick of pine to the god of the kitchen stove, it's only right that my permission be sought. If you really want me to leave for the time being, those are my conditions—all the better not to work for this family. His taunting words confounded them. Don't think I don't know. Compared to last year, the number of houses this family owns has increased, and rumour has it that their revenues have doubled. Oh, it's risible! Just where do you intend all that money to go, exactly?... What can I say? The road to hell is paved with good intentions. After all, many a fire has started at home, and what is your eldest son, if not a ball of fire? I'll have your fortune soon enough, and then I'll show you what a real New Year's party looks like, he boasted, having decided already how he would treat his penniless friends down in Isarago and where they would spend New Year's Eve drinking.

He's back... his sisters whispered, fearing him like a boil that threatened to burst at any moment. Their readiness to heed Ishinosuke's every demand only emboldened his wilfulness.

Water! Water! he cried out, collapsing by the *kotatsu*. Truly, his deplorable manners were without peer. Despising him in her heart, his stepmother cursed her obligations to the boy; but even so, she swallowed her words of reproach and instead said: Here, I've brought you a blanket and a pillow, lest you catch your death. I have to go now and prepare the dried anchovies for tomorrow, since I can't very well trust the maids not to let any go to waste. If you want a job done properly… Thus stressing her own frugality, she left the spendthrift to his hangover. As noon approached, O-Mine was growing more and more anxious about the promise she had made to her uncle. With no time to gauge her mistress's mood, she took the first free moment she had to remove her kerchief and went to see Mrs Yamamura. About that little matter I mentioned the other day, she ventured, wringing her hands. I hate to ask at such a busy time, but I promised I'd try to find the money by noon today. Your help would mean so very much to both my uncle and me. We'd be forever in your debt. When O-Mine had first broached the matter, her mistress had been non-committal. Still, her reply of I don't see why not had given O-Mine some cause for hope. Since that day, however, O-Mine had refrained from pressing the matter further, fearing that mistress's fickleness might scupper her chances. But now, with the promised noon fast approaching, O-Mine had begun to worry. Had the mistress forgotten? Why hadn't she said anything? It felt awkward to bring up something important like this again, but the desperation of her situation had pushed her to come out and say it. The mistress, however, assumed only a look of amazement and surprise. What on earth are you talking about? Although, now that you mention it, you did say something about a sick uncle. And about borrowing some money, yes? But surely I never said I'd lend it to you myself? No, you must have misunderstood me. I'm sure I never said anything of the kind! Too late did O-Mine realize that this had been her mistress's ploy all along. Truly, what a cruel trick to have played on her!

The Yamamura daughters were turned out beautifully for the forthcoming festivities, their magnificent kimono adorned with designs of cherry blossom and willows suggesting all the natural beauties of the season to come, the splendour of these robes set off by the fine silk under-robes and collars and layered skirts that had been bought for the occasion. The mistress delighted in seeing her girls arrayed so handsomely and was keen to show them off—if only it had not been for their brother getting in the way. Such extravagance, of course, was hardly in keeping with her ethos of frugality. Would that he would just go! that he would disappear! she had to stop herself from saying aloud. Her distemper, however, could not be contained: were a wise bonze to have looked into eyes, he would have seen her engulfed in flames, her body in a cloud of black smoke, and her mind in a fury. Meanwhile, all this talk of debts and money merely poured more oil onto the fire. Of course, she recalled intimating that the girl could have the money, but how loath she was to make good on that promise now. You must have misheard me, she said curtly, cutting short the conversation. To draw the matter to a close, she blew rings of smoke in the air, feigning ignorance.

Was it really so much to ask for? All of two yen? And after she herself had even agreed to it! She can't have gone senile in these last ten days... Suddenly, her eyes alit on the drawer of the writing chest. There was bound to be an untouched stack of notes there—ten, maybe twenty yen's worth. Two notes were all that was needed to make her uncle happy, to put a smile on her aunt's face, and to ensure that little Sannosuke would have some *zōni* for New Year's. She just had to get her hands on it somehow. Though filled with bitter resentment towards her mistress, O-Mine, much to her own frustration, was powerless to say anything; meek and obedient by nature, she simply lacked the means to prevail on anyone. As she stood there in the kitchen, crestfallen, the thunder of the noonday gun rang out, reverberating in her breast.

Mother, I beg you, please come at once! The message had come from the mistress's daughter, who had gone into labour that very morning. It was her first child, and her husband was panicking, uncertain what to do. In the house, with nobody more experienced to hand, there was pandemonium. You must come right away! the message implored, for a first birth is always a matter of life and death. There was a rickshaw waiting to take the girl's mother to her residence in Saiō-ji, and, seeing as this was New Year's Eve, there was no time to lose. Yet she was in two minds. There was money in the house, and her prodigal stepson was still sleeping off his hangover—she could not be in two places at once to keep an eye on things. In the end, her love for her daughter won out, however, and so she clambered into the rickshaw, burning with resentment that her husband, that poor man's Duke Tai of Qi, had decided to go fishing on today, of all days.*

On her way out, the mistress passed Sannosuke. After several failed attempts, the boy had finally managed to locate the Yamamura house in Shirokane. Conscious now of his own shabby appearance, he did not want to embarrass O-Mine, so he timidly popped his head around the kitchen door. Who's there? she called out, turning to hide her face as she wept by the stove. Yet she knew that it was her cousin. But what was she to say to him? She could hardly say, I'm so glad to see you! I won't get told off for coming in, will I, O-Mine? Sannosuke asked. Did you get the money? Father made me promise to thank the Yamamuras properly. Blissfully unaware of what had gone on, the boy's face was beaming. Oh, what agony it was for O-Mine to behold! Just wait here a minute, she said. There's something I need to do first. With that, she dashed off to check the house. The daughters were all in the garden, engrossed in a game of battledore and shuttlecock, the errand boy was still out, while the seamstress was upstairs—and besides, she was deaf, and so would pose no problem—and, when she checked, the young master was still

* According to ancient legend, Duke Tai of Qi (also known as Jiang Ziya) would fish without bait, letting the fish come to him of their own accord.

sound asleep by the *kotatsu* in the living room.* She pressed her hands together and entreated the Shinto gods and Lord Buddha himself that they might forgive her for what she was about to do, for, reluctant though she was, she had no choice. If anyone is to be punished, O Lord, let it be only me, she prayed. Even though they'll be the ones using the money, my aunt and uncle know nothing of what I'm about to do, so please forgive them. Sacrilege though it is, please allow me to steal this money! In a daze, not quite knowing whether this was a dream or waking, she grabbed two notes from the bundle that she had spotted earlier in the drawer of the writing chest, handed them to Sannosuke and sent the boy on his way. Oh, but what a fool she was to think that not a soul had witnessed the whole episode…

As nightfall approached, the master returned from his fishing trip, the living image of the god Ebisu.† His wife followed soon after. Relieved by the safe delivery of her grandchild, she was kind even to the rickshaw driver who had ferried her back. I'll return just as soon as I've finished seeing to everything here this evening, she said. And tell them I'll send one of my daughters over to help in the morning. Then, thanking the man for his efforts, she gave him a tip. Heavens, there's so

---

* Battledore and shuttlecock was a beloved pastime often played by girls around the New Year.

† The Japanese god of fishermen and luck.

much to do! What I'd give for another hand. O-Mine! Have you boiled the mustard spinach already? Has the herring roe been washed? Is that husband of mine back yet? Then, lowering her voice, she asked, And what about that boy of his? Is he still here? When she was told that he was, she frowned.

That evening, Ishinosuke seemed subdued. There's nothing I'd like more than to stay here for the next three days, ringing in the New Year with you all, but you know I just can't help myself. It's such a bore having to make small talk with all those hordes of people who'll come to pay their respects, dressed up in all their finery. I'm tired of being lectured to as well. And besides, there aren't any pretty faces among our relations, so I haven't the least inclination to see them. At any rate, I've promised my chums from the back streets that I'd meet up with them tonight. In fact, I really ought to be on my way. We'll celebrate some other time. Now, I wonder how much the old man will give me. He seemed rather pleased with himself earlier... Yes, all in the hope of money had he lain in bed all day since morning, waiting for his father to come home. Buddhists do say that children are the shackles of the three realms, but how especially hard the parents of wayward children have it. These unbreakable bonds of blood are such that, no matter how much a child probes the depths of depravity, no matter how far into the abyss they fall, society will never pardon you if you abandon them. And so it was that Mr Yamamura, in order to preserve the family honour, found it necessary to open the doors of his precious storehouse, much to his shame and regret. Counting on this, Ishinosuke had told his father that there was a debt that had to be repaid that very evening, that he had undertaken to act as a guarantor for a friend of his and even signed his name, and that, if the aforementioned friend couldn't get the money to those thugs in the gambling den, there would be trouble—like a house of cards, he said. Besides, it would mar the family name, let alone his own, he added. So, in a word, the money was essential. It was just as his stepmother had feared. How many times?! She was vexed by her husband and his leniency, and yet she was also well aware that Ishinosuke could run rings around them with his silver tongue: he could not be dealt with as easily as she had seen off O-Mine that morning. With a fearsome look in her eye, she kept glancing over at her husband to see whether his face had registered the gravity of the situation, but the man merely stood up and walked quietly over to the safe, from which he extracted a bundle of fifty yen. I'm not doing this for your sake, he said, handing the boy the money. I'm doing it for your sisters who are still unmarried. Just think of the damage that could be done to their reputations if rumours were to spread. You could ruin your eldest sister's husband's reputation, too. For generations, this family has been honest, respectable, upright. Scandal has never so much as touched the House of Yamamura! But you—you're the reincarnation of the demon Tenma!* A wrong 'un like you

* According to Buddhist tradition, the demon of the sixth heaven in the realm of desire, who tries to prevent people from doing good.

has enough lack of foresight to go and steal money right out of another man's pocket—and, mark my words, it will bring shame on us for generations to come! Important though it is to me, I'd much rather see my fortune squandered than the honour of my family. This won't mean anything to a good-for-nothing scoundrel like you, but ordinarily I'd expect you, as the young scion of the Yamamura family, to be helping me make our New Year's calls—not subjecting us publicly to rumour and insinuation. You're a damned disgrace of a son to make your aged parents weep like this! Oh, it's a sin! You read enough when you were little to be able to tell the difference between right and wrong, so how has it come to this? Get out of my sight! Just go! I don't care where! And see that you don't bring any more shame on this house! His tirade over, the old man slunk off, leaving his wayward son to slip the money into his breast pocket.

Goodbye, Mother! A very happy New Year to you! I'll be off then, he called in an affected tone of voice as he made to leave. O-Mine! My *geta*, if you please! the voice issued subsequently from the vestibule. I'm leaving. Then, sweeping the girl aside, he stepped out into the street and headed who could say where? The tears shed by his father would soon be forgotten, like a dream glimpsed on a night of revelry and debauch. What have I done to deserve such a profligate son? the old man mused. And what have I done to deserve such a wife, who raised the boy in his profligacy?... There was no salt with which to purify the room, but, the moment Ishinosuke was gone, they had it swept clean all the same. The boy's departure came as a relief: hard though it had been to part with the money, it was harder still to bear the sight of him, and so they rejoiced now at his absence. How could he have become so shameless and impudent? How I should like to see the face of the woman that brought him into the world! his stepmother thought, sharpening her tongue as usual. O-Mine, meanwhile, was oblivious to what was going on, terror-stricken after the crime that she had committed. Had she really just done that? Had it not all been a dream? Surely she was bound to be found out? They'd be able to tell right away if even a single note were missing from a stack of ten thousand. And if the precise amount that she had requested had disappeared, would suspicion not immediately fall on her? It was only natural. And what would she do if they did find out? What would she say? Lying was a sin. Yet if she confessed, the blame would fall on her family, too. She was ready to take responsibility for her own misdemeanour, but doing so would stain her honest uncle's reputation indelibly. Such was the way of things for the poor. People would be quick to draw their own conclusions and judge him. Oh, how wretched it all was! But what could she do? She even considered whether her own suicide might keep her beloved uncle from harm… Though she followed the mistress about her work, her mind kept returning to the writing chest.

That night, accounts were settled, and what money was left in the house was gathered together and sealed with the family insignia. At the very last moment, the mistress remembered the twenty yen that Tarō the roofer had repaid. O-Fude! O-Mine! Bring me the writing chest, she called out from her room. There it was! Her fate, too, was about to be sealed. O-Mine resolved that she would go and tell the master everything, right from the very start, with neither artifice nor stratagem—even how the mistress had been so cold-hearted. The truth would protect her. She would not try to run away or hide; rather, she would confess, telling them that it was not greed that had led her to steal and that her uncle had no part in it. Then, if they would not listen to her, she would have no choice but to bite her tongue clean through and bleed to death on the spot. She would risk her life to make them see the truth—but as she made her way to the back room, mustering the courage to do just that, she felt like a lamb being led to the slaughter.

O-Mine had taken only two notes. That meant that there ought to have been eighteen left. But when she opened the writing chest, the entire bundle was nowhere to be seen. She turned the box over and shook it, but to no avail. Even more curious was that out of a drawer fell a single scrap of paper with a note on it that had been written God knows when:

I have borrowed the monies in this drawer, too.

Your humble servant,
Ishinosuke

They all looked at one another in astonishment. That scoundrel! But O-Mine was now in the clear. Had Ishinosuke taken the money in ignorance of her guilt? Or had he in fact known her crime and committed one of his own so as to cover it up? If the latter, it would have made of Ishinosuke the girl's guardian deity. Who is to say what happened next…

GROWING PAINS

(Takekurabe)

I.

BY THE GREAT GATE of the Yoshiwara there stands a weeping willow, where sybarites and rakes are wont to pause on their journeys home, gazing back on that floating world with a sense of longing and regret. And though the path that threads there around the quarter is as long as the trailing branches of the willow itself, yet the dark waters of the moat bounding it—waters as black as the teeth of those beauties kept within its high walls—reflect not only the play of lamplight but also the laughter and music that spill out from the upstairs parlours in those grand houses of assignation—all so tantalizingly close that one could practically reach out and touch it.* The rickshaw traffic bearing fares to and from this site of splendour flows continuously, no matter the hour—day or night—a presage of the unmeasurely fortunes that are made there. And for all that the neighbourhood

* The practice of blackening the teeth, known as *o-haguro*, was common among women of marriageable age until the twentieth century. Because of its associations also with prostitution and the licensed quarter, the moat surrounding the Yoshiwara came to be known as the 'Tooth-Black Ditch'.

behind the Yoshiwara might bear the rather pious-sounding name of the Daion Temple Precinct, it too is, as the locals will aver, a rather lively spot—yet, once you turn off at the Mishima Shrine, you will see nothing nearly so impressive, but only row after row of down-at-heel tenement houses, all with sagging eaves and rain shutters that scarcely half close. Nobody would claim that business exactly thrives here. Outside these dwellings, people craft queer-looking paper cuttings, daubing them with white paint and then skewering them on sticks, making them look like *dengaku* tofu, and not just the odd house here and there, but everywhere!—people solemnly hang them out to dry in the morning sun and take them in again at dusk, entire households engaged in their manufacture. Should anybody happen to ask what they are, Fancy not knowing! the astonished reply will come. Why, they're frames for *kumade* charms.* Come the Day of the Rooster in the eleventh month, the greedy and the grasping vie to get their hands on them at the Ōtori Shrine. How terribly superstitious those merchants are! From the moment the New Year's pine decorations come down, every true man of commerce will spend the remainder of the year making them. Even the part-timer who takes it on as a sideline will find his hands and feet bespattered with paint from the summer months on, depending as he does on the proceeds to cover the garments

* *Kumade*, literally meaning 'bear paw', is also the Japanese word for a rake. Here, the term denotes a stylized good-luck charm made in the shape of rake and heavily adorned, the idea being that they will help business owners to 'rake in' money and good fortune.

he must buy for New Year's. O Lord, he implores the mighty deity enshrined at the Ōtori, if you grant mere buyers of these charms such riches, then deign to grant us makers of them ten-thousand-fold profits! Are those prayers ever answered? I wonder. Never have I heard talk of anyone getting rich in these parts… Most of the residents here have some connexion to the licensed quarter. The men do odd jobs for the smaller, less-reputable houses, and you can always hear their clutch of shoe-check tokens jangling at their waists. In the evenings, as the sun begins to set, you will see them in the doorways of their houses, donning their *haori* as they leave for work, the wife's face peeping over the husband's shoulder as she strikes a flint behind him for luck. Could this be our last farewell? she frets. Tensions run high in the Yoshiwara, after all: a dozen bystanders might easily be slain amid a lovers' quarrel, and Heaven help the man who dares to thwart the love suicide of a courtesan and her paramour. Oh, yes! the resentments can be perilous. It's a dangerous business, you see; but still, off the men trot, as though heading to a picnic. The girls, too, are put to work: she might start off on the lowest rung, as a maid to some courtesan in one of the great houses, or else, with paper lantern borne aloft, she might ferry clients between one house and the next, but, as she trips along, rushing to complete her training, what future awaits her? Certainly not a glamorous one spent in the limelight, as she imagines to herself. Soon enough, she'll find herself in her thirties, a woman of refined years and respectable form, neatly arrayed in a simple striped-cotton kimono set with a pair of plain indigo *tabi* under some sensible leather-soled *geta*, bustling smartly along with a bundle under her arm (one need hardly say what it is). There she goes, clattering up the pier to the back door of the teahouse, where she complains, It's too far to go all the way around. Is it all right if I just leave this here? Yes, quite so: the bespoke-work woman, as the locals call her. The ways and mores of the Yoshiwara are indeed different from other places. Few are the girls here whose *obi* is tied neatly at the back. And while it may be one thing for a woman of a certain age to relish a bold pattern and an egregiously wide sash, yet the very sight of a saucy little thing aged fifteen or so, decked out in this get-up and holding a winter cherry in her mouth, is quite enough to make some avert their eyes.* Perhaps it cannot be helped in a place such as this. One day you might hear of a girl in one of the third-rate knocking shops taking the name Murasaki Something-or-Other, dressing herself up as a heroine from *The Tale of Genji*, only for her to run off the very next day with some local hoodlum and open a night stall selling *yakitori*. Neither will know the least thing about business, of course, and so, having diced up and burnt through their assets, just like the chicken they sold, they'll find themselves penniless soon enough, and she longing to return to the coop she has flown. And yet, there are those who will think the girl awfully romantic and far more appealing than

* According to folk tradition, winter cherry (*Alkekengi officinarum*) is believed to prevent pregnancy or even bring on miscarriage.

any ordinary woman—there is, as the saying goes, no accounting for taste. Naturally, this has its effect on the children here, too. One need only look to the procession down the Yoshiwara's main thoroughfare during the Niwaka Festival each autumn: to see the speed and skill with which the little ones learn to imitate the famous jesters Rohachi and Eiki would astonish even Mencius' mother.* Praised for their talents, the boys will go around that very evening, reprising their roles. Such shamelessness begins at the tender age of six or seven—but just wait until they are fourteen! You'll see them come strutting down the street on their way back from the bathhouse, a towel slung over their shoulder as they hum some licentious tune. Truly, their precocity is a frightening thing. The songs they sing at school, too, are liable to take on the jaunty rhythms of the quarter, just as any sports day is apt to turn into a festival dance with all manner of chants and rituals. Education is a difficult enough undertaking as it is: pity the poor teacher who has to cope with all that! And not far from the quarter is the Ikueisha, a private school with close to a thousand pupils, all crammed into its narrow classrooms cheek by jowl. Despite this overcrowding, the teachers there are held in the highest esteem, and, for the locals, the word 'school' alone is enough to conjure thoughts of the Ikueisha. Among the many children who attend this school, some are the sons of firemen,

* The mother of the sage Mencius (*c.*371–*c.*289 BCE), who took such pains over her son's education, is held up in East Asian culture as a paragon of motherly devotion.

and, even without being told, they are clever enough to know that their fathers are stationed at one of the drawbridges in the Yoshiwara.* Playing at firemen, they clamber up ladders to the top of the spiked bamboo fences used to keep thieves out. Hey, you've broken one of the spikes! one of them will whine. Now another boy, the son of a bogus lawyer, will launch his cross-examination: Your father's a bagman, isn't he? To hear his father's sorry profession laid out in such plain terms now makes the poor boy blush a deep crimson. And lest we forget the pampered sons of the patrons of these brothels, lodged in simple dormitories and free therefore to affect the airs and graces of nobility. What a dash they cut as they promenade in their scholar's cap and expensive Western clothes, and yet how comical to hear the obsequious cries of Sire! Sire! follow after them… Yes, among these hordes, there was, from the Ryūge Temple, a child by the name of Nobuyuki. How many years were left before his thick black hair would be shaved off and he would don the immutable black trappings of a bonze? Did he feel the vocation in his heart? Or had he perhaps merely resigned himself to following in his father's footsteps? Who can say? At any rate, the boy, like his father, was a scholar. He was quiet by nature, and his reticence had at one time irked his classmates,

---

* There were, at the back and sides of the Yoshiwara, other entrances used as alternative routes in emergencies or else to leave the quarter without passing through the Great Gate; the drawbridges themselves folded in half, with nails driven into the underside to prevent their being used by the women of the quarter to escape.

who would respond by playing cruel jokes on him. Once they had even strung up a dead cat and shouted, Here, this is your line of work! Why don't you give it the last rites? But all that was in the past now. These days, he excelled at school, and nobody dared to look down on him, not even for a moment. All of fourteen, he was of average height, but his cropped hair, which looked like a chestnut in its burr, set him apart from the others, and while his name, Fujimoto Nobuyuki, may have been ordinary enough, yet there was something in his bearing, a certain quality that bespoke a disciple of the Lord Shakyamuni.

2.

That year, the festival of the Senzoku Shrine fell on the twentieth day of the eighth month. On this red-letter day, floats from every neighbourhood compete to climb the embankment of the moat, practically storming the Yoshiwara itself. The spirit of youth here is palpable. Only do not be fooled by the pullers' tender years: they may be young, but, having learnt so much on the streets already, these children are wise to the ways of the world. Yes, they may be smartly turned out in matching kimono, but they have conspired to make as much mischief as possible today. Just you wait and see… The leader of the young group of hoodlums who had dubbed themselves the Back Street Gang was a boy of fifteen called Chōkichi. His father worked as a fireman, and, ever since the boy had stood in for him as a policeman during the Niwaka

Festival, wielding his iron baton with relish, he had been full of swagger: he wore his *obi* rakishly low now over his hips, and looked down his nose at anyone who had the temerity to ask anything of him. Truly, he cut an abhorrent figure. If he weren't the chief's son, you know... the other firemen's wives were wont to whisper behind his back. Arrogant and prideful, the boy indulged his every whim, far exceeding his station, but then, one day, he met his match in a boy called Shōtarō. Although three years his junior, this boy from the high street, the grandson of the pawnbroker Tanaka, came from wealth and was well liked. Moreover, whereas Chōkichi had to make do with the Ikueisha, this Shōtarō attended the more prestigious public school—and although the two of them might well sing the same songs, Shōtarō always relished pulling a wry face, looking down on the other as on some poor relation. Over the last two years, Shōtarō's gang had managed to attract a few grown-up boys into its ranks, and they had won renown by well and truly trouncing Chōkichi's during the festival. Though Chōkichi was less prone to picking fights nowadays, his reputation would be on the line if he lost again this year. If ever anybody challenged him, his usual riposte—I'm Chōkichi, from the Back Streets!—risked sounding like empty bravado. And when the time came for the swimming race across the Benten ditch, he might even struggle to find people to join his team. In terms of strength alone, he was sure to win, but everybody had been taken in by the Tanaka boy's goody-goody demeanour, to say nothing of his considerable intelligence—and this was yet another worry. Worse still was that some of his own boys—Tarokichi and Sangorō, to name only a couple—had gone over to the other side. With only two days left before the festival, it was looking ever more likely that Chōkichi's gang would lose once again. Beside himself with despair, Chōkichi decided to mount an offensive. What did it matter if he lost an eye or a leg, just so long as that Shōtarō got what was coming to him. If only he could recruit Ushimatsu, the rickshaw-puller's boy, or Bunji, whose father made paper hair-ties, or even Yasuke, the toymaker's son—that would show him. Or better still... Yes, why hadn't he thought of it before? Of course! Fujimoto could lend them some smarts! And so, as evening fell on the eighteenth, Chōkichi found himself picking his way through the densely packed bamboo grove of the Ryūge Temple, and, from there, strutting over to Nobuyuki's room, where he poked his head in and, swatting away the mosquitoes that swarmed around his face, called out, Hey, Nobu! Are you there?

Listen, I know people call me a thug, Nobu. But so what if I am? What's done is done. I can't very well go and change the past. But look here! It all started last year when that pipsqueak from Shōtarō's gang decided to pick a fight with my little brother during the lantern festival. Quick as a flash, they all jump the lad and—can you believe it?—smash up his lantern. They tossed him in the air, and one of them even shouted, Not so brave now, are you? And that's not all! The *dango*-seller's boy they call Donkey, that great brute who goes around acting as though he's a grown-up, starts bad-mouthing me to my brother, saying, Calls himself the head of the gang, does he, your brother? More like the arse end, if you ask me. That's it, the arse end! Meanwhile, I'm off hauling the float towards the Senzoku, so I only hear about all this after the fact. Well, I was ready to go and get even there and then, but my old man won't hear of it! Gives me a ticking-off, so he does! I practically had to cry myself to sleep! And then there was the year before that! You'll remember how those high-street brats got together by the paper shop and started putting on a skit or something. When I went over to have a look, they started giving me cheek, saying, Don't you Back Street kids have your own games? And there they all were, bowing and scraping before Shōtarō... Well, I'm not one to forget a slight, believe you me! He may have money, Nobu, but he's just the grandson of some two-bit loan shark. Where does he get off, acting like that? I could beat the kid to a pulp. And d'you know, I'd be doing the world a favour getting rid of scum like him. Well, this time, I'm going to get my own back on him, no matter what it takes. Be a pal, Nobu, come on! I know you can't stand violence, but I need your support. We have to avenge honour of the Back Streets! And besides, don't you want to teach that stuck-up Shōtarō with all his airs and graces a lesson? You know, when they call us all dunces from the Ikueisha, you're no exception... Won't you please help us? I'm begging you. Just carry one of the lanterns at the procession, that's all I'm asking. If I lose again, I'm done for! Chōkichi was so filled with rage that his broad shoulders were trembling. But I'm not strong like you, said Nobuyuki.

That doesn't matter! I can't even carry a lantern! Then you don't have to. But what if I join and you still lose? If we lose, we lose. So what? What matters is that you'll be there with us. If you give it a bit of swagger and let them know whose side you're on, it'll boost our morale. I may not know much, but I know you're a smart kid! If those other lads start showing off and hurling big words at us, you'll be able to hit back with a bit of Chinese. There, that's more like it! What a mercy. Having one of you on our side is like having the strength of a thousand. Say, thanks, Nobu!... Such endearments were not in the boy's everyday vocabulary.

These two boys could not have been more different: one the son of a labourer, with his child's *obi* and slip-on straw sandals; the other reminiscent of a priest, in his sombre brown-calico *haori* and purple waistband. Ordinarily, they would have clashed, but, what with Chōkichi's having been born practically on the steps of the temple, he was doted on by the priestly boy's mother and reverend father, too, and, what with their both being looked down on for the school they attended, perhaps there was more to unite the two of them than first met the eye. Yes, it was a pity that Chōkichi did not have a more likeable temperament, but then he had never been one to attract others, not like Shōtarō, who had a winning personality and even had the backing of the older boys in the neighbourhood. But Nobuyuki had no illusions. Whatever happened, the blame for Chōkichi's losing would rest squarely on Shōtarō. This favour had been asked of Nobuyuki, and his sense of duty would not allow him to refuse. Very well, he said, I'll do it. I'll join your gang. I mean it. Just try to avoid violence if you can. Then again, I suppose it's unavoidable if they come at us first. All the same, when push comes to shove, I can make short work of someone like Shōtarō. Having forgotten all about his weakness, Nobuyuki extracted from the drawer of his desk a fine Kokaji dagger that he had been brought as a gift from Kyoto. He showed it to Chōkichi, who peered at it in wonder and said, Careful now, you could really cut someone up with that... Still, I'll bet it's easier to carry than a lantern.

3.

Her hair, which, if let down, must surely have reached all the way to her ankles, was gathered up neatly, and her fringe swept back into a large bun. The style, though given the fearsome-sounding appellation of a 'red bear', was popular among the young ladies of good family. Her skin was fair, her nose lovely and straight, and her mouth, although perhaps on a little on the large side, was pleasant to behold when closed. Taken individually, her features were far from those of a typical beauty, yet her voice was soft and clear, her inquisitive eyes were full of gaiety and allure, and her lively demeanour was most agreeable. I'd pay to see her in three years' time, the young rakes would say as they stumbled out of the Yoshiwara in the early hours, spotting her on her way back from the bathhouse. And truly, she cut a magnificent figure, her towel slung over her shoulder, and her throat gleaming white above her persimmon-coloured *yukata* with its bold motif of butterflies and birds, worn with a two-tone black-satin *obi* tied high around her waist, and, on her feet, a pair of tall lacquered *geta*, of a kind rarely seen in the neighbourhood. Her name was Midori, and she belonged to the Daikoku-ya. A native of Kishū, her words had a slight, though charming, southern lilt. What endeared her to others most of all, however, was her spirit of generosity. True, the amount of silver she raked in was extraordinary for a child of her age, but then her older sister was one of the Yoshiwara's prized courtesans, now at the height of her prosperity, and so Midori, too, benefited from this. Hoping to curry favour with her star attraction, even the madam of the house would give Midori some money every now and then and tell her go and buy herself a doll, while the new apprentice girls might say, Here, take this. It isn't much, but it should be enough to buy a ball. Such gifts, moreover, were bestowed freely, without any expectation that the recipient should show too much gratitude for them. Midori, likewise, would think nothing of buying twenty matching rubber balls for all her school chums, and she was known on occasion to delight her friend the brush-maker, whose wife ran the paper shop, by buying up all the shop-soiled toys and amusements on their shelves. Such extravagance, day after day, night after night, was not at all commensurate with Midori's age or station. What was to become of her? Though she had both her parents, they were wont to overlook this behaviour and never so much as uttered a word of reproach. It was certainly odd how the owner of the brothel indulged her so. Yet if one were ever to question her motives, one would learn soon enough that the girl was no adopted daughter or even any distant relation. When her older sister was being sold to the house, the owner, who had come to appraise her, invited the girl and her parents to come and seek their fortune in the capital as well, and so the three of them had packed their bags and donned their travelling clothes. Whatever else might have gone on in the background, they now kept house for the owner; the mother also taking in sewing for the girls and the father moonlighting as a book-keeper for one of the third-rate establishments in the quarter. Meanwhile, Midori herself was sent off to learn music and dancing—the arts of pleasure—as well as sewing and embroidery; the rest of the time, she did as she pleased, spending half the day in her sister's room, and the other half playing in the streets, her eyes and ears assailed by drumming and *shamisen* music set against the twilight vermilions and dusky purples of the quarter. When she first moved to the neighbourhood, the other girls had called her a country bumpkin and poked fun at her for wearing a wisteria collar with her lined kimono. For three days and as many nights, she sobbed her heart out. But now the shoe was on the other foot. You look like a peasant, she would offer bluntly, leaving her poor victim speechless. With the festival now set for the twentieth, her friends were hounding her with suggestions for things to do. Do whatever you like, she replied. How about we all come up with something that everybody can enjoy? Don't worry about the cost of it. I'll pay for everything, she added, throwing caution to the wind as usual. How apt children are to know a good thing when they see it—indeed, they were hardly likely to encounter such beneficence in a sovereign of theirs again. Let's put on a skit, one of them said. We can rent a shop somewhere, where everyone passing by can see us! Don't be ridiculous! a boy wearing a twisted headband hit back. What we really need is money to build a *mikoshi* to carry through the streets! A real one! Like the one they have on display at back of the Kabata-ya. It doesn't matter how heavy it is—a few heave-hos and away we go! But that's no fun for us! a group of girls interjected. Why should we have to stand there, watching you lot shout and sweat? Besides, you wouldn't get much enjoyment out of that now, would you, Midori? We'll go for whatever you pick… Curiously enough, the girls seemed to be hinting that they would rather skip the festival altogether and go off to the Tokiwa-za theatre for an evening of light entertainment. Suddenly Shōtarō's irresistible eyes lit up. How about a magic lantern show? I've got some slides at home. Midori can buy whatever we're missing, and we can do it by the paper shop. I'll run the lantern, and Sangorō can be the narrator. Can we, Midori? What do you say? I like it! she said. And with Sangorō doing the narration, everybody will be splitting their sides laughing. Maybe we can even get his face put on one of the slides! Wouldn't that be hilarious? And so it was that Shōtarō was entrusted with buying the necessary items. How comical he looked running around, drenched in perspiration! Word of their plan got around, and, finally, on the eve of the festival, it reached the back streets.

4.

Hear the beating of the drums, the twang of the *shamisen*! Though the Yoshiwara overflows with music all the year round, a festival is something unique. And, truly, the Day of the Rooster, when all the local shrines compete with one another in splendour, is an unparalleled red-letter day in the calendar! Each gang wore matching cotton kimono with the character of their street printed on the back. (Though some did grumble that this year's kimono were not a patch on the ones they had last year.) Their sleeves were tied up with flaxen *tasuki* that had been dyed a sunny yellow with gardenia—the flashier, the better, naturally. For the little ones who were not yet fourteen, there were *daruma* dolls, papier-mâché owls and dogs, and countless other toys and trinkets; and they would boast about how many they had managed to collect—seven, eight, nine, eleven, even!—while bells great and small jingled on their backs as they dashed about gamely in their *tabi* alone, unshod. Shōtarō stood apart from the group, cutting a dash in his emblazoned livery coat with its red stripes, his navy-blue apron set off against the pallor of his neck. A second look revealed the subtle turquoise of the *obi* drawn tightly across his waist, the exquisite over-dyeing of the silk crêpe, and fine print-work that had made the beautiful markings on his collar. A sprig of flowers taken from a float adorned the back of his headband, and though the clacking of his leather-soled *geta* echoed in time to the drumbeat, yet he kept his distance from the music-makers. The eve of the festival had passed without incident, and now, as the sun began to set on the great day itself, twelve of them gathered by the paper shop. The only one missing was Midori, who was still applying her evening make-up. What's taking her so long? Shōtarō wondered, pacing restlessly in and out of the shop door. Go and fetch her, Sangorō. I don't suppose you've ever been to the Daikoku-ya, have you? Just call her name from the garden. She'll hear you, all right. Run along, now, hurry! If you say so. But I'll leave my lantern here; I don't want anybody stealing the candle. Watch it for me, will you? Blimey, you're a tight bastard, aren't you? Anyway, get a move on. You could've run there and back already... The lad did not seem to mind being scolded by a boy his junior. In the words of Jirozaemon, he said, I'll be back.* With that, in the blink of an eye, he went bounding off. Is that Idaten, the fleet-footed deva incarnate, I see before me? one of the boys quipped. Given the way Sangorō fairly flew, it was little wonder the girls laughed, watching him go. He was a stocky little thing, with a hammer-shaped head and

* The reference is to Sano Jirozaemon, a man said to have been a wealthy patron of the licensed quarter, and who around the turn of the eighteenth century, in a notorious incident known as the Hundred Slayings in the Yoshiwara, went on a killing spree, cutting down dozens of prostitutes with his sword. In a popular adaptation of the episode for the kabuki stage, which premiered only a few years before the composition of this story, Jirozaemon tries to abscond over the rooftops.

hardly any neck, and, when he turned his head in profile, it revealed a protruding forehead and a snub nose—and left no doubt as to why his nickname was Bucktoothed Sangorō. His complexion was unquestionably dark, but what struck one most was the look of mischief in his eyes and the charming dimples he had in his cheeks. And, dear me, his eyebrows almost covered his eyes, as though they had been pinned on in a parlour game played blindfolded, lending him a curious look of innocence. Poverty meant that he had to wear a plain cotton kimono with tight sleeves that day,* but to his unsuspecting friends he simply declared, I didn't have the time to have a matching one made. The eldest of six, he was the son of a rickshaw-puller who could scarcely make ends meet. True enough, he could always find a dependable stream of fares on the stretch of teahouses leading up to the Great Gate,† but the wheels of his conveyance never quite managed to keep pace with his household expenses, which forever sped away from him down the path to financial ruin. Twelve's plenty old enough to help earn a crust, the boy's father had told him the year before last, and so he had sent the boy to work at the letterpress printer's in Namiki. However, the boy had turned out to be bone idle and did not even last ten days there. Ever since then, he had never once held down a job even for a month. He had spent the

* Tight sleeves, the better to work in.

† These teahouses were popular as sites from which potential clients could be introduced to the brothels of the Yoshiwara.

last two months of the year making shuttlecocks part-time at home, then in the summer he had lent a hand to the ice-seller by the Inspection Office.* His distinctive voice was good at drawing in customers—a real asset, as his boss had remarked. Last year, he had pulled one of the floats during the Niwaka Festival, but his friends had teased him about it, saying that it was it a job fitter for those clowns who came from the slums of Mannenchō—and the memory of it, as well as the nickname, had stuck. Everybody knew that Sangorō liked to play the clown, and nobody could hold it against him: that he was well liked was his sole asset. The pawn shop that Shōtarō's lot ran was a veritable lifeline for Sangorō and his family, and their gratitude was no small matter. Yes, the daily interest rates they charged may have been exorbitant, but were it not for them and the money they loaned, disaster would have struck at any moment, and so they could hardly begrudge them. Hence, when Shōtarō invited him to join his gang, the boy had felt duty-bound to accept. All the same, Sangorō had been born and raised in the back streets, the land he lived on belonged to the Ryūge Temple, and even the house they lived in was the property of Chōkichi's father. He could hardly turn his back on all this. Still, he had made his bed, and now he had to lie in it—no matter how hard it was for him… Shōtarō went inside the

* The Inspection Office and neighbouring hospital, both situated to the rear of the Yoshiwara, were where the prostitutes of the licensed quarter were legally obliged to submit themselves for, respectively, the testing and treatment of sexually transmitted diseases.

paper shop and sat down to wait for Midori, and, to while away the time, he began to sing 'The Hidden Ways of Love'. Well, well, we'll have to lock up the ladies around this one, won't we? the owner's wife laughed. The boy flushed scarlet around his ears. Trying to cover his embarrassment, he called out in a loud voice, Come on, you lot, let's go! before running straight out the door and into his grandmother. Shōtarō! Why aren't you home for tea? Too busy playing, no doubt. Haven't you heard me calling you all this time? You can play with your friends again after you've had your tea. Then, turning to the brush-maker's wife, Thanks, I'm sure. Left with little choice but to do as he was told, Shōtarō was marched home. The gang was only one person fewer, but how sad and lonely they now felt. Even the older ones were sorry to see him go—not because he played the clown, cracking jokes like Sangorō did, but rather because it was a rarity to encounter such a nice and amiable young lad who came from money. Cor, did you see her? The old bag's sixty-three if she's a day, but just look at her all made up like that. It's a wonder she doesn't still paint her face. You should hear how she purrs like a cat when she recoups her loans. They say she doesn't even care if the man's croaked! She'll be right there at the funeral with her ledger. I wouldn't be surprised if she ended up planning a love suicide with her money, trying to take it with her into the hereafter. The way we're forced to bow and scrape before the likes of her, that's money for you! Still, I wouldn't say no to it. I hear even some of the big houses in the quarter borrow from her... Thus, standing there, gossiping in the middle of the road, did the women take stock of the widow Tanaka's fortune.

5·

Even the brazier seems cold on long nights spent waiting, as the old song has it. Such are the ways of love. That evening, however, the summer breeze blew cool and invigorating. Having washed away the heat of the day, Midori now readied herself in front of a full-length mirror. Her mother was seeing to it personally that her daughter's hair, tangled now after the bathhouse, was retouched properly. I know she's my own child, she thought to herself as she viewed the girl from every angle, but what a beauty she is! You need more powder at the back of your neck, she said. The girl had on an unlined silk kimono that had been dyed a refreshing pale blue, the colour of water, and over it a slightly narrow white-tea-coloured *obi* flecked with gold. It would be some while before they could even think about lining up her options for footwear on the flagstone in the garden… As he paced back and forth, Sangorō wondered what on earth she could still be doing. He even had time to make half a dozen circuits of the perimeter wall, and had yawned more times than he could count. The area was infamous for its mosquitoes, and no sooner would he swat them away than they would instantly reappear, biting his neck and forehead. Just as he was reaching his wits' end, Midori materialized. I'm ready! she said. Without a word of reply, he grabbed her sleeve and dragged the girl off, running. I can hardly catch my breath, and I've got a pain in my chest, she complained. If you really are in such a hurry, then go on ahead. What do I care? Arriving then at the paper shop separately, they learnt that Shōtarō had gone home for wafer cakes sandwiched with adzuki-bean paste. Well, this is no fun! No fun at all! We can't very well put on the magic-lantern show without him… Do you sell tangrams? she asked, turning to the shopkeeper. Or even a board game would do. We need something to entertain us, she said despondently. I've just the thing! said the lady. Borrowing some scissors, the girls set about cutting out the pictures from the book they were given, while the boys all gathered around Sangorō to rehearse their dances for the Niwaka Festival.

Come and see the quarter flourish!
Lights and lanterns at each door,
People thronging every street…

Their singing may have left much to be desired, but their recollections of the festival in recent years were so fresh that they could still remember all the words and moves, gesturing and clapping perfectly in time to the rhythms. Wondering what all the commotion was, a crowd of people began to gather at the shopfront, watching the dozen or so boys. Among them, a voice shouted out, Is Sangorō in there? Come quick, it's urgent! It was Bunji, the son of the man who made paper hair-ties. I'll be there in a jiffy! the boy shouted back and nimbly dashed out across the threshold, unsuspecting of what awaited him. Take that, double-crosser! the voice said, as a fist struck him squarely in the face. That's what you get for sullying the name of the Back Streets! You'll rue the day you ever made fun of Chōkichi and his gang! Dumbstruck, Sangorō tried to make a run for it, but one of the boys grabbed him by the collar and stopped him. Kill him! Somebody, get Shōtarō, too! Don't let that coward get away! And just where do you think you're going, Donkey? Their cries rose up like a swelling ocean wave, poised to wreak havoc at any moment. Suddenly, the lanterns dangling from the eaves came crashing down. Mind the hanging lamps! cried the brush-maker's wife. No fighting in front of the shop! But for all her protests, no one was listening to her now. There must have been well over a dozen of them. One, wearing a twisted headband, hurled a large lantern into the fray, after which all manner of punching and trampling ensued. Truly, this was rampageous behaviour! But the one person they were looking for—their enemy, Shōtarō—was nowhere to be seen. Where's he hiding? they demanded, ganging up on Sangorō. Where's he run off to? You won't tell us? Is that it? Punches and kicks rained down on the poor boy. You think we're going to let him get away just like that? Unable to bear it any longer, Midori pushed past those who tried to stop her. What's poor Sangorō done to deserve this?! she pleaded. If it's Shōtarō you want, then save it for him! He didn't run away, and he's not hiding either! He simply isn't here! This is our spot, and I'm not going to let you lay a finger on it! You really are a rotter, Chōkichi! What are you beating him up for? There, he's lying on the ground again! If you want to pick on someone, pick on me! Come on, hit me! I dare you! The brush-maker's wife tried to hold her back. Let me go, damn it! she cried, struggling to free herself. You're all mouth, you little whore! Following in that tramp of a sister's footsteps like some beggar! Take this, bitch! said Chōkichi, stepping to the front of the crowd, taking off his muddy sandal and lobbing it at the girl. His aim was true: with a loud squelch, the sandal hit Midori square in the forehead. Her face dropped. Don't, you might get hurt! said the woman, holding her back. Get a load of that! What a sight! Chōkichi gloated. Oh, and by the way… Nobuyuki's come over to our side, so we'll be ready for you any time you want to get even. You dimwits! You cowards! You sissies! We'll be ready and waiting. Mind how you go in the dark now, not least in the back streets!… Then, just as Sangorō was knocked to the ground once more, they heard footsteps running towards them. It was the police! Somebody had ratted on them. Let's get out of here! shouted Chōkichi. Scattering to the four winds, Ushimatsu, Bunji and the dozen or so others ran off to what must have been their hiding places in the back alleys. You bastards! Sangorō called after them. Chōkichi! Bunji! Ushimatsu! Damn you and you and you! What are you afraid of?! Come out and kill me, why don't you! Just try it! I dare you! And even if you do, I'll come back as a ghost and get my revenge! Mark my words, Chōkichi! The boy broke down in a fit of sobs, hot tears scalding his cheeks. Battered and bruised, his body must have been in agony. His little sleeves were torn all over, and his back and thighs were covered in dirt and grit. Frightened by the ferocity of this uncontrollable outburst, the others now gave him a wide berth. Only the brush-maker's wife ran over to him and took him in her arms. There, there, she said, as she brushed the dirt off his back. There were so many of them. And they were stronger than all of us. Even the bigger boys couldn't have done much to help. It wasn't a fair match, I know. Still, you're lucky you weren't badly hurt. I don't want you going home alone, though—they might be waiting for you yet. To be on the safe side, let's ask this nice policeman to take you home, shall we? You see, officer, what happened was this... After a brief summary of the events, the policeman took the boy by the hand and said that he would gladly see him home. Sangorō protested, however. No, I don't want you to come with me, he said, cringing. I can make my own way home. Now, now, there's nothing to be ashamed of! said the policeman. After all, I'm only doing my duty. Don't you worry, lad! He smiled and patted Sangorō on the head, which only made the boy cringe further still. But my father will be furious if he hears I've been fighting. The father of one of those other boys is our landlord. As he spoke, there was a glum look of resignation on his face. Well, we don't want you getting in any trouble, now, do we? said the policeman. I suppose I could see you just as far as the door in that case. With that, the policeman led him off, much to the relief of the others, who watched them go... But what was that? Just as the two of them reached the corner, Sangorō shook free of his chaperone and ran off as fast as his legs would carry him.

6.

How peculiar! It would have been less extraordinary to see snow falling under the blazing summer sun, but still, Midori had made it abundantly clear: she was in no mood to go to school that day. Well, if you don't fancy any breakfast, why don't I order in some sushi for you later? suggested her mother. You don't have a fever, so I doubt you've caught a chill. It must have been all that excitement yesterday that's worn you out. Why don't you stay here and let me visit the shrine for you this morning? But Midori was having none of it. No! she protested. She had to go and pray for her sister's prosperity. It wouldn't feel right, she said, not going herself. If you give me some money for the offertory box, I'll be back before you know it. Off she ran, out the door and to the Inari shrine that stood among the rice fields down in Asakusa. There, she rang the gong shaped like a crocodile's mouth and clapped her hands together in supplication. But what was it that she asked for? All the way there and back, along the path between the rice paddies, Midori hung her head. Spotting her in the distance, Shōtarō called out to her as he went running over. I'm sorry about last night, Midori, he said, clutching at her sleeves. But you've got nothing to be sorry for, she replied. All the same, I'm the one they were after, I'm the one they wanted to fight. If it hadn't been for my grandmother, I'd never have gone home, and Sangorō wouldn't have taken such a beating. I went to see him this morning, you know. He was still upset about it, still sobbing. It made me sore enough to hear him sob like that, but then he told me that Chōkichi threw his sandal in your face! That bastard's gone too far this time. Forgive me, Midori! I didn't run away on purpose! I wolfed down the food, but then, just as I tried to leave, Grandmother said she was going for her bath and told me to keep an eye on things at home. The ruckus must have happened while she was out. I really didn't know anything about it, I swear! he apologized profusely, as though for a sin that he himself had committed. Does it hurt a lot? he asked, glancing up at her forehead. Nothing that won't pass with time, she said, smiling sweetly. But if anyone asks, Shōtarō—anyone at all—you mustn't let on that Chōkichi threw his sandal at me. I'd get into such terrible trouble if Mother found out. Neither of my parents has ever so much as laid a finger on me. If they discover that I got my forehead covered in mud from Chōkichi's sandal, they'd be so angry. It would be as if he'd trampled over me with his own feet! The poor girl turned her face away. I really am sorry, Midori. It's all my fault. Please, forgive me. I can't bear to see you like this. What you need is some cheering up. By this point in the conversation, they were already nearing Shōtarō's house. Why don't you come in for a bit, Midori? There's nobody else at home. Grandmother's out, making her rounds. It gets so lonely here all by myself. I can't bear it. Come on, I'll show you those woodblock prints I was telling you about. We have all kinds of them, he said, still clutching the girl's sleeve, refusing to be parted from her. Midori simply nodded her head in agreement. They went in through a rustic-looking concertina door that led into the garden. The garden itself was a modest affair, but there were lovely bonsai all lined up in little pots, as well as a weeping fern hanging from the eaves, which, if memory served, Shōtarō had bought at the fair held on the Day of the Horse. Those who did not know any better would have been puzzled, however. Here was the house that belonged to the richest family in the neighbourhood. Only two people lived there—the grandmother and her grandson. Myriad keys hung about the old woman's waist, keeping her belly and legs constantly chilled, and, whenever she went out, neighbours in the tenements all around would keep watch over the place, so, naturally, nobody ever attempted to break in. Shōtarō went on ahead and chose a spot where there was a pleasant breeze. Won't you come and join me? he said, suavely offering Midori an *uchiwa*. He was, perhaps, a little too precocious for a boy of merely twelve. He showed her one woodblock print after another, all of which had been in his family for generations, and it gave him tremendous pleasure to hear Midori admire them. Would you like to see an antique battledore? he asked. It belonged to my mother. She was given it when she worked as a maid in a stately mansion. Isn't it funny? Just look how big it is! And to think how different people's faces looked back then. Oh, I wish she were still alive, my mother… She died when I was two. My father's still around, but he went to live in his family's house back in the countryside, so now it's just me and Grandmother. I wish I had a family like you do, Midori… Come on, boys don't cry, said the girl. Careful, now, or you'll get your prints all wet. Maybe I am just a sissy. Sometimes I do wonder... True, not so much lately, but back in the winter, when I had to do the rounds in Tamachi, I'd find myself going down to the embankment of an evening and just crying. There were so many times when I did that. And not because of the cold, either. I didn't mind that so much. But for some reason—it's a mystery even to me—I'd think about all kinds of things. I began doing those collections the year before last. Grandmother's getting on, you see, so it's dangerous for her to go out at night. Her eyes are starting to go, too, and she sometimes has trouble putting her seal on the receipts. There used to be quite a few men helping her, but she said they were lazy and taking us for fools because we were just an old lady and a kid. When I'm a little bit older, we're going to reopen the pawnshop. Even if things won't be exactly the way they used to be, I still can't wait to hang the board with the family name on it outside. Other people call my grandmother a miser, but it's all for my sake that she's so careful with money. I can't help feeling sorry for her. While I'm out collecting in places like Tōri-shinmachi, I meet a lot of people who are hard up, and I'm sure they must say horrible things about her. Just thinking about it makes me want to cry. Oh, what a sissy I am! When I went to see Sangorō this morning, the poor sod was in so much pain, but he just carries on working because he doesn't want his father to know what had happened. When I saw that, I was speechless. It's not right for a man to cry, is it? That's why those horrible lads from the back streets were making fun of him. Shōtarō blushed, apparently ashamed of his own sensitivity. There was a sweet innocence about him as he tried to avoid Midori's gaze. You looked so smart at the festival yesterday, you know. You even made me jealous of all the boys and their clothes. Smart?! Me?! he retorted. You should have seen yourself! You were the best-dressed girl there. Everybody said so. You looked beautiful—more beautiful even than all the famous ladies of the quarter! We all said so. If you were my sister, I'd be so proud of you. I'd follow you around everywhere and brag about you to everyone. After all, I don't have any siblings of my own. Say, why don't we go and have our picture taken? I can put on what I wore for the festival yesterday, and you can dress up in that striped silk kimono of yours. We'll go over to Katō's in Suidōjiri and have him take it. Won't that kid from the Ryūge Temple be jealous! Oh, that'll really make him angry. He'll be seething! He'll be so jealous that he'll turn green from all that bile! Then again, maybe he'll just laugh at us. Well, I don't care even if he does. We'll have a big picture taken, and then Katō can use it as a poster for his business! Why the long face, Midori? Wouldn't it be funny if you pulled that for the picture! he said. Don't you like the idea? But what if my face *does* turn out funny in the picture? You might go off me then... Midori's sweet voice pealed with laughter. Shōtarō's mission to cheer her up had succeeded.

The coolness of the morning had passed, giving way to the heat of the aestival sun. Come and see me again this evening, Shōtarō! We can light the lanterns in the garden and chase after the fish, Midori said as she was leaving. The bridge over the pond's been fixed, so there's nothing to worry about now. Shōtarō watched her go in a state of euphoria. Now, there was a beauty!

7.

Nobuyuki of the Ryūge Temple, and Midori of the Daikoku-ya: they both of them attended the Ikueisha. Earlier that year, around the end of the fourth month, when the cherry trees had already scattered their blossom and, under the shade of new green leaves, the wisteria began to flower, the school had put on its spring sports day in the fields of Mizunoya-no-hara. So engrossed were they all in the tug of war, and the games of catch and skipping, that they scarcely noticed the sun set on that long day. That evening, for some reason, Nobuyuki was not his usual well-composed self, and by the edge of the pond he stumbled over the root of a pine, landing on his hands and knees on the red-clay path and covering the sleeves of his *haori* in dirt. What a mess he looked! Midori, who happened to be passing by, took pity and offered him her crimson silk handkerchief. Here, she said, wipe yourself down with this. One of Nobuyuki's friends had witnessed this display of solicitude, and began to burn with jealousy. Don't you find it odd? he whispered. For all Fujimoto's saintly ways, he looked more than happy talking to the girl, and you should have seen the way he smiled as he thanked her! Maybe he means to marry her. She's setting her sights a bit high, though, isn't she? A trollop like her? She'll have to mend her ways a little if she wants to become the mistress of a *temple*… Nobuyuki had never been able to abide gossip. He disliked hearing people being talked about in that way and would always turn aside, a look of repugnance written upon his face. What forbearance he must have needed, then, finding himself the subject of such idle chatter! From that moment on, the mere mention of Midori would be enough to strike fear in his heart and bring on palpitations. It was an indescribably unpleasant feeling. And yet, he could not permit himself to fly into a rage each time this happened. Insofar as possible, he would try to feign ignorance or indifference, wearing a wry expression and hoping that the discomfort would soon pass. Sometimes a well-chosen word or two was necessary to put an end to it, but still, the embarrassment would linger after every confrontation, and he would be left standing there forlorn, sweat dripping down his back. Oblivious to these things at first, Midori would call out to him in her usual friendly way as she went home after school. One day, she was walking ahead of him and stopped to admire some unusual flowers growing by the side of the road. She waited for him to catch her up. Look at the beautiful flowers! she said. They've got such long stalks, but I still can't reach them. Pick some for me, will you, Nobu? You're tall enough. He had been singled out. What was he to do? He could hardly just walk on and leave her standing there. But he was also acutely aware of what his younger classmates would be thinking, and the more he thought about it, the more he cringed. He plucked the ones closest to hand with no regard for their quality, and then, sheepishly, he practically threw them at her before carrying on. Such examples of his boorishness astounded Midori, but as they grew in frequency, it began to seem as though he were being deliberately unkind. To nobody else did he show such poor treatment. If she tried to ask about it, he would brush her off. If she tried to get close to him, he would flee. And if ever she spoke to him, he would grow cross. He was sullen and brooding, and it was impossible to cheer him up. Well, thought Midori, if he wants to be like that, then so be it. It's perverse being so angry all the time. Clearly, he's no friend of mine, so what's the point even in trying to talk to him? Even so, Midori was rather put out by all this. Now, if ever they happened to pass one another in the street, they scarcely acknowledged one another, let alone stopped to talk. In the blink of an eye, a vast river had stretched out between them, and now, as if ferrying between the two banks had been forbidden, they each followed their own separate path along the shoreline.

The day after the festival ended, Midori suddenly stopped attending school. There was hardly any need to ask why. Though the mud had been easy enough to wash off her forehead, the shame of the incident had proved indelible. The children from both gangs sat crammed together in the same classrooms, and so there should have been nothing to set them apart, yet, as ever, a sharp division persisted. Chōkichi's behaviour on the night of the festival had been despicable. What kind of a coward would pick on a poor, defenceless girl and take advantage of her weakness? The boy's ignorance was rivalled only by his wanton violence, but had it not been for Nobuyuki, he would never have dared to be so bold as to start a ruckus in the high street. Oh yes, that Fujimoto boy might have pretended to be all meek and mild in public, but he was bound to be the one pulling the strings behind the scenes. So what if he was more senior at school? So what if he was clever? So what if the Ryūge Temple was to be his one day? Midori of the Daikoku-ya hadn't taken so much as a scrap from him. And he had the temerity to call *her* a beggar! She didn't owe him anything. Who cared that the great and the good went to pray at his temple, when, for the last three years, among her sister's patrons there had numbered bankers and stockbrokers! Why, a member of parliament had even offered to buy her out of bondage and make her his wife—until, that is, her sister decided that she did not much like the little man's attitude and turned him down. But he was an eminent man, all the same! All the madams in the quarter said so. Ask them yourself if you don't believe me! Yes, had it not been for Midori's sister, the Daikoku-ya would not be the fine establishment that it was, and the owner wouldn't have been half as nice to Midori and her parents. Just take the incident with his beloved porcelain statuette of the god of wealth, which always sat in the *tokonoma*. One day, while batting a shuttlecock around in the parlour, Midori knocked over the vase beside the statuette, which toppled over and smashed it. When it happened, the owner, who had been drinking in the next room, merely said, For a girl, Midori, you're really quite spirited, aren't you? and not a word of reproach. Had it been anyone else, his rage would have been beyond compare. Such leniency, which derived ultimately from her sister's success, made her the envy of all the maids. Yet if she was a mere keeper of her master's house, still her sister was Ōmaki of the Daikoku-ya—and so, no, she did not have to put up with insults from the likes of Chōkichi. Nor was she content to let herself be bullied by some would-be bonze from the Ryūge Temple. School no longer interested her. Everyone had underestimated just how wilful this girl could be. In a fit of pique, she broke her stylus, dashed her ink to the ground, and dispensed with all her books and her abacus. Who needed school when you could lark around with friends?

8.

How impatiently the rickshaws fly into the Yoshiwara by evening, and how lonely they seem as they trundle off at dawn, carrying with them dreams of the night before. One gentleman pulls his hat down over his eyes, while another, seizing a handy kerchief, masks his face. Heaven forfend that another should recognize him. The exquisite agony of that parting blow lingers in his body still, and the more he thinks back on it, the greater the bliss he feels. What an uncanny sight, that grin upon his face! He'd better watch his step when he reaches Sakamoto—those vegetable carts on their way back from the early-morning markets at Senju are a menace. And not for nothing is the stretch as far as the turning by

Mishima Shrine known as the Madman's Highway, where the solemnity of those august, dignified faces melts away and, dare I say, there isn't a single stiff upper lip to be seen. They may well be considered men of rank and quality somewhere else, but, my goodness, there are those who will stand at the crossroads here and not hesitate to deem these men worthless. One need not draw on *The Song of Everlasting Sorrow*, nor on the exploits of that daughter of the House of Yang, who famously won the Emperor Xuanzong's favour, to show that there are times when daughters are more valuable than sons. It is a common enough story, the girl from the dark slums of the back streets growing up to become a fair and radiant princess. There was one just recently—a beauty who took the snow-clad name Yuki and moved to a certain upmarket house in Tsukiji, where now, renowned for her skill in dancing, she entertains wealthy noblemen and all sorts.* These days, she passes the hours in parlours, asking the most naïve-sounding questions like, What tree does rice grow on?, as though she had grown up in the lap of luxury, when only yesterday she was dressed slovenly and earning a living making playing cards in some back room not far from the Yoshiwara. She enjoyed quite the reputation around here, but, as the saying goes—out of sight, out of mind. Her fame has been eclipsed now by one of the dyer's younger daughters. A flower

* Tsukiji was the location of Tokyo's foreign concession, the implication here being that the girl, likely working in the newer Shin-Shimabara licensed quarter, would entertain both Japanese and foreign clients.

of a girl from Senzokumachi, she is the pride of the New Ivy, the house where she has taken the name Kokichi. All their lanterns burn for her, and they thank their lucky stars to have found such a rare specimen grown in native soil: no common or garden variety she. From dawn till dusk and back again, the gossip one hears is concerned only with the success of girls. Boys, it would seem, are neither here nor there; wastrels of little more use than some black-spotted mutt sniffing around in the rubbish for scraps. At sixteen—the age of impudence—the young swains of the neighbourhood, as they like to be known, band together in groups of five or six, and while they have not yet mastered the samurai's swagger or the affectation of tucking a flute into their *obi*, yet they will still pledge fealty to a leader who, for whatever reason, invariably goes by some solemn-sounding sobriquet, and cut about, sporting lanterns and matching headbands. But before you know it, they will have learnt the ways of rolling dice and bantering with the girls that they peruse behind the latticework when they go window-shopping, daring now and then to make the odd ribald joke. Tending diligently to the family business is a matter for daylight hours only, and, having gone off to the bathhouse of an evening, they come strutting back in their *geta* and ill-fitting kimono. Have you seen the new girl over at the Such-and-Such House? She looks like the girl in the haberdasher's over in Kanasugi, only her nose is twice as flat… Yes, these rogues have only one thing on their mind. At every window, they pilfer tobacco and pinch tissues, and they cherish as the honour of a lifetime the playful slaps they receive in chastisement for this. Why, here even the odd young scion of a respectable family has been known to style himself as a local thug and start picking fights with people by the Great Gate. Behold! the power these girls have, the gay thronging of the quarter which knows no season! Though the old processions are going out of fashion nowadays,* the soft echo of the slippers worn by the serving girls at the tea-houses is music enough to the patrons' ears, punctuating the rhythms of song and *shamisen*. And still, when you ask the stream of people who come flooding merrily into the quarter what it is that they hope to find there, the answers come: scarlet collars, flowing robes, ornate hairstyles, smiling lips, twinkling eyes, and so on… So hard is it for them to put their finger on what exactly they find so alluring. Yet the mere knowledge that a woman is a courtesan is enough to instil reverence around here. It must be seen to be believed… Surrounded by all this, day and night, no wonder, then, the white of Midori's robes came to be stained red. The men, as she saw it, posed no threat or danger, and she did not consider the women's profession anything improper. Those tearful farewells with her sister back in the village of her birth were but as a dream now. How she envied her sister, at the top of her game and able to support her mother and father! Yet she knew nothing of the many sorrows and hardships that her

* High-ranking courtesans would once process through the streets of the licensed quarter, accompanied by attendants, lantern-bearers and musicians. These elaborate affairs, which advertised the house for which the courtesan worked, began to fall out of fashion in the Meiji era.

sister's work entailed: all she heard were those little mousey squeaks her sister gave as she tried to draw in customers and that tapping on the latticework as she whispered incantations for good luck, and all she saw were those mysterious strokes on the back that she gave her clients as they departed. Proficient now in the vernacular of the quarter, Midori used it without any shame wherever she went—alas. It was a sorry sight. She had just turned thirteen. To see the way she cradled her dolls and pressed their cheeks together, one might have taken her for a nobleman's daughter; as far as she was concerned, lectures on morality and all those lessons in domestic management were best left for the schoolroom. Gossip was what now bent her ear around the clock, who was in and who was out, talk of kimono, of the fine bedding given as gifts and piled high outside the house as a mark of its prosperity, and of the tips given to teahouses for introducing new patrons. Anything that was loud and showy was deemed beautiful, and anything that was not was thought hideous. The girl was too young to discriminate and was incautious in what she said. Whichever flower her inexperienced eye alighted on always seemed to her the fairest. Impulsive and unruly, she ran about as she pleased, her head forever in the clouds… Madman's Highway. Drowsy Lane. The gentlemen revellers pass this way in the early hours. At last, this neighbourhood of late risers has finished its work for yet another day. The sweepers and water-sprinklers have left their telltale design of waves along the high street, but just look out over it and you will see them coming through the gates in their droves already, coming after nesting awhile in the slums of Mannenchō and Yamabushichō, in Shintanimachi and its environs—each with his own skill. One might call them entertainers (for want of a better word): see the candy man with his little drum, the acrobats, the puppeteers and jugglers, the tumblers and lion dancers. They all have their own distinct costumes—and for every elegant robe of silk and gossamer, one is bound to find a washed-out cotton kimono with a Satsuma splash, a thin black-satin *obi* holding it in place. Men and lovely ladies, groups of five, seven, ten, even, and the lone, wizened old man, all skin and bone, clutching under his arm a battered old *shamisen*. And look over there, a girl of four or five, her sleeves tied up with a bright red *tasuki*, being made to dance the Kinokuni. Among their best patrons are the men who tarry in the quarter, the better to escape their troubles at home, or the melancholy beauty in need of some diversion. It is a fact well known that you can make enough money to last a lifetime in the Yoshiwara. Those who make the journey there have no time for the paltry sums they might find in the outlying districts—oh no, even the most dubious-looking beggar, his tattered hems reminiscent of seaweed, knows better than to pause by the entrance, and instead just heads straight inside. A minstrel goes by, her pretty face concealed by the straw hat she wears tilted daringly forward, giving only an enticing glimpse of her cheeks. Her voice and her hands are so famed that the brush-maker's wife clicks her tongue when she sees her. What a pity, she says, that none of us ever gets to hear that voice! Fresh from her morning bath, Midori sat fixing her hair with a boxwood comb as she perched on the front step of the shop, watching this motley crowd pass by. Why don't we call her over, Auntie? Before the woman even had the chance to reply, Midori had run up to the minstrel and slipped something into the veritable net that was her sleeve—this she did with the utmost discretion, of course—and swiftly brought the pet songbird back and had her perform her favourite song.* By and by the minstrel took her leave, her dulcet voice pronouncing a humble request for future patronage, knowing full well how unlikely that would be. What a lovely thing to have done! the crowd that had gathered around exclaimed in astonishment. And a mere child, too! They seemed more pleased with Midori than with the minstrel herself. Imagine if we could stop all the entertainers here in the street, Midori said, turning to Shōtarō, and have them sing and dance and strike their drums and play their *shamisens* and flutes! We'd finally see all the things we never get to see them do! However, sooner taken aback than taken by this bold suggestion, Shōtarō replied bluntly: Forget it!

9.

Thus have I heard… The sound of those austere voices chanting the sutra, borne on the breeze that swept through the great

* The song named in the original, 'Akegarasu' ('The Morning Call of the Crow'), is a *jōruri* narrative piece from the Edo period, telling of the love suicide of a prostitute at the Ivy in the Shin-Yoshiwara.

pines in the temple grounds, ought to have blown the dust of earthly cares from the heart as well—yet it also carried wafts of smoke from the fish being grilled in the monks' kitchens and the smack of infants' nappies that had been set out to dry on the gravestones. And while there was nothing strictly wrong with this, at least not according to religious doctrine, yet, in the eyes of those who would rather their bonzes dwelt on matters loftier, all this had too worldly a pungency. There was, at the Ryūge Temple, an abbot whose belly had grown fat in proportion to his means. It was truly a sight to behold. What words of praise might be offered up in the hope of describing his complexion? No cherry-blossom pinks or peach-blossom cardinals; no, his entire head, from the top of his freshly shaven pate all the way down to the nape of his neck, shone evenly like burnished copper. And when he would raise aloft his bushy eyebrows, now flecked with white, and fairly roar with laughter, even the Buddha in the Great Hall risked being so startled that he might have fallen from his altar. The abbot's wife was comparatively young; only a few years past forty, she had a fair complexion, and thinning hair tied up in a neat little bun, and was really quite presentable. She was always gracious to the devout, and even the acid-tongued woman who ran the flower stall just outside the temple gate would never have dared to say a bad word about her—her heaven-sent reward, no doubt, for all those hand-me-downs and leftovers she gave to charity. A member of the laity originally, she had lost her husband early on in life, and, with nobody else to turn to and nowhere else to go, she had come to the temple, offering to work there as a seamstress. Consequently, in return for keeping body and soul together, she took over the laundry and the cleaning, too, and before long she was preparing the meals there as well. Seeing her industriousness (she even helped the monks with the ritual cleaning of the graves), the economical abbot did his sums and was quick to offer his sympathies. The gulf of twenty years separating them gave her pause. Some might even have called it shameful. But what choice did she have? And besides, there were worse places to live out her days. In the balance, she decided, it was better not to worry too much about what others thought. She was a good woman at heart, and so, scandal or no scandal, it was not for others to reproach her. When she fell pregnant with her first child, a girl who would be named O-Hana, it was the kindly retired oil-dealer, Sakamoto, who intervened—to say that he played the go-between would be something of a stretch—urging them to do the right thing and tie the knot. Later, she gave birth to a brother for the girl, Nobuyuki. And while he may have been a pious, eccentric boy, who spent all his days holed up in his room, his sister O-Hana was precious little thing with smooth skin and a round chin, and, while nobody would have called her a great beauty, yet she did not lack for prospective suitors. It seemed a pity to let her talents go to waste, but then it would hardly have done to set up such a respectable young girl—the daughter of an abbot, no less!—as a geisha. Things might have been different in a world where the Lord Shakyamuni himself had played the *shamisen*, but, alas, not in this one—and so, out of a sense of propriety, they instead had a pretty little tea shop built on a street in Tamachi, where they installed the girl so that she might purvey her charms from behind the counter. Young men who knew little about measures and even less about prices soon began to loiter around the shop, and never did the stroke of midnight ring out without at least one or two customers still hanging around. Busiest of all, however, was the abbot himself—collecting loans, inspecting shops, officiating here and there; there were sermons to be preached any number of days per month, accounts to be made up and gone over, sutras to be read. He would wear himself out if he was not careful, and so every night, at dusk, he would lay his floral-patterned mat out on the veranda, take a seat and cool off, half naked, with a fan, as he poured himself a brimming cup of *awamori* and, lover of fish that he was, ordered a tray of *kabayaki* to be brought from the Musashi-ya in the high street. It was of course Nobuyuki whom he would send out to fetch the delicacy for him—A large fillet, mind!—and the boy dreaded it every time. He would walk along, his eyes fixed firmly on the ground, hoping to avoid the group of children gathered at the paper shop on the corner opposite. It pained him to think they might see him and comment.* As a precaution, he would always trot nonchalantly past the entrance to the eel

---

* The requirement for Buddhist clergy to remain celibate as well as to abstain from eating meat and fish was lifted shortly after the Restoration in 1872; however, social taboos on these practices persisted.

shop, and then, when the coast was clear, double back and dart inside. Never had he so much as dreamt of touching the foul comestible himself.

Nobuyuki's father, the abbot, was a practical man, a man of the world even, although in some quarters this had led to his developing a reputation for avarice. He was not, however, the timid sort liable to be swayed by gossip, and, if ever he found himself with a free hand, he was not above fashioning *kumade* charms himself. Why, he was even known to open a stall on a vacant lot outside the temple entrance for the Day of the Rooster, where he would put his wife in a headband and have her sell them alongside hairpins, calling out, Roll up! Roll up! Get your good-luck charms here! At first, she had thought it all a little unseemly, but her fears were soon allayed when she heard about the roaring trade done by mere amateurs up and down the strip—to say nothing of their vast profits. Besides, amid all the bustling hoards, nobody would even spot her, and after dusk, what chance was there then? During the day, she could have the woman who ran the flower stall help out, and then as soon as night fell, she could go down and hawk the things herself. Was this greed? she wondered. At any rate, her former reticence was no more, and, before she knew it, she found herself hounding down customers to cries of Discounted! Going for a song! Buffeted by waves of humanity, the buyer would stand there, dazed and confused, quite forgetting that he had already come to the temple market only two days ago to provide himself for the hereafter. Three lucky hairpins for seventy-five *sen*!

Her price so named to allow for haggling, the man will try to knock her down. Make it five for seventy-three, he'll say, and you've got a deal!… In a pitch-dark world there's many a way to turn a shady profit. Nobuyuki found such thoughts truly distressing. Yet even if word of the stall didn't reach the parishioners, those in the neighbourhood might still speculate. And what if the other children at school got wind of the fact that Nobuyuki's mother was running a stall right in front of the temple and was selling hairpins with that crazed look on her face? It would be mortifying. Might it not be better to put a stop to all this? he quietly suggested, but the abbot simply roared with laughter. Button it! he said dismissively. It's none of your business, I'm sure… Prayers by morning, and accounts by evening. As his fingers worked the abacus, the abbot's face beamed in exultation. The very sight of it was repugnant to Nobuyuki. Why had his old man ever bothered to shave his head? the boy wondered, full of bitterness and reproach.

Born to a close-knit family and raised in a nest of tranquillity, there was scarcely cause for the child to be so morose. He was a rather timid creature, though, and whenever he did speak, it passed more often without notice. His father's enterprises, his mother's conduct, his sister's upbringing—it all bespoke some kind of mistake. But nobody would listen to him, and so he resigned himself to a melancholy, mournful silence. Let his acquaintances think him sullen and perverse: at heart he knew he was a mere milksop. He lacked the courage to confront anyone who spoke ill of him, no matter how trivial the slight. Instead, whenever he heard those cruel words, he would retreat to his room and, in cowardly fashion, avoid all contact with the outside world. His academic excellence, coupled with his respectable background, meant that nobody yet had guessed his shameful secret. Some of classmates had even been heard to say, That Nobu's a right cold fish.

10.

On the night of the festival, Nobuyuki had been sent on an errand to his sister's in Tamachi, and so it was not until later, after he returned home, that he learnt of the unimaginable that had transpired outside the paper shop. When he heard the details from Ushimatsu, Bunji and the others the next day, he found himself shocked by Chōkichi's violence, but what was done was done, and it was too late now for disapproval. He was outraged that his name had been invoked without his knowledge, and although he had taken no part in what had gone on, he felt in a way personally responsible for the trouble they had caused. Did Chōkichi feel at all ashamed for his actions? Perhaps. Knowing full well that he would likely get a tongue-lashing from Nobuyuki, he avoided him for several days. Finally, though, things cooled down. I know you're going to be angry with me, Nobu, he said, but you weren't there, you didn't see how it was! I'm sorry. How was I to know you wouldn't be there? or that Shōtarō had done a runner? I didn't exactly *plan* to beat up Sangorō or pick a fight with that bitch! But once people start swinging lanterns, there's no going back. We were just trying to have a bit of fun. It was all my fault, I accept that. I should have listened to you, yes, but there's no sense getting angry about it now. With you behind us, we felt like big shots! You can't abandon us now. So you've got a problem with what happened. I get it. You be the leader, then! That way, we won't put a foot wrong next time!... No, I couldn't, not even if I wanted to, Nobuyuki wanted to reply, but Chōkichi had set aside his pride, and his apology was too grovelling to refuse. All right, he said, I'll do it. But if you go around picking on the likes of Sangorō and Midori, you'll only disgrace yourselves. Wait till Shōtarō has his crew with him. And don't go picking any fights in the meantime... Though he did not scold Chōkichi too harshly, he prayed that he would be spared another brawl.

Sangorō had been the innocent party in all this. They had kicked him and beaten him with abandon, and for days afterwards the poor boy could neither sit nor stand on account of the pain he was in. Each evening, his father would take his empty rickshaw and head off to the teahouses of the Yoshiwara. What's happened to that Sangorō of yours? his acquaintance the caterer asked him, almost with suspicion. The boy's looking awfully feeble these days, isn't he? But Sangorō's father was known as 'Umble Tetsu, and never once had he been known to challenge his betters. Yes, it went without saying that the wealthy patron of the quarter could make whatever unreasonable demand of him he pleased, but then so could his landlord. Little wonder then that when he found out that the boy had been fighting with

Chōkichi—of all people!—he chastised him, exclaiming, But he's our landlord's son, for heaven's sake! I don't care if you were in the right and he was in the wrong, you mustn't fight with him. Go and apologize this instant! Go on! Oh, what a foolish thing to have done! You astonish me, boy, you really do… It was unavoidable now that Sangorō would have to go grovelling before Chōkichi, but the boy merely gritted his teeth and got on with it. As the days turned into a week and more, his resentment faded along with the pain he felt, and before long he was happily babysitting Chōkichi's brother again, carrying the infant around on his back and singing it lullabies, all for the princely sum of two *sen*. Sangorō had now reached that impudent age of fifteen, but, not in the least abashed by his bulky frame, he would go strutting down to the high street, where he always ended up bantering with Midori and Shōtarō. What, are you a wet nurse now? they asked, seeing the baby. They were still great friends, though, for all that they teased him.

The riot of cherry blossoms in spring gives way to the dazzling array of lanterns lit for Tamagiku in summer.* By and by, the autumn festivals fill the quarter with rickshaws—in one street alone, you might see seventy-five fly by in a mere ten minutes. But then, before you know it, the show is over. Meadowhawks begin to dart over the rice paddies, and it is

---

* Tamagiku was a celebrated courtesan, who was murdered by a young samurai in 1726. Lanterns were lit ritually throughout the Yoshiwara during the sixth lunar month to commemorate her death and console her spirit.

almost time for the quails to start calling on the embankments of the moat. Morning and night, the autumn winds cut through you. At the variety shop, mosquito repellents have made way for pocket warmers. The sound of the millstone grinding flour at the old *sembei* shop by the Stone Bridge has taken on a desolate quality. From the clocktower of the famed Kadoebi, the chimes now seem to carry a note of pathos. And, in the distance, the fires of Nippori burn without cease, their glow forever visible on the night horizon no matter the season, yet only now do the people mark their smoke with sorrow.* You follow the narrow path along the embankment behind a teahouse and hear the plaintive strains of a *shamisen* drifting down like rain. Your love shall be my blanket, the geisha sings as her skilful hands pluck their pitiful tune. Ask any courtesan who has served out her time in the quarter, and she will tell you: it is not the frivolous tourist who begins to frequent the Yoshiwara in this season, but those faithful few who hold a deeper connexion to the place. But, oh, how they do like to gossip here! It would be tedious to enumerate all the talk, but one thing I will tell you: in the Daion Temple Precinct, an extraordinary thing happened. A blind masseuse not even twenty, full of unrequited love, they say, and bitterness for her plight, drowned herself in the pond at Mizunoya. That was a tale worthy of the telling. But others, devoid of such sensation, will fail to arouse much interest—such as when the greengrocer's boy, Kichigorō, was asked what had

* A reference to the crematorium at the Yanaka Cemetery.

become of Takichi, the carpenter's lad, who seemed to have vanished off the face of the earth. He was picked up for a bit of this, said Kichigorō, miming a gambler dealing out cards. And that was the end of it… Over on the main road, you will see a group of children holding hands and singing something like 'Ring a Ring o' Roses'; even their innocent play seems quiet at this time of year. The only noise in the quarter is the unceasing clatter of rickshaws.

It was the kind of desolate night when, no sooner do you start to wonder how long the autumn rains will go on drizzling than their gentle patter is drowned out by a thunderous downpour. Not reliant on passing trade, the brush-maker's wife closed her doors towards evening. There, as usual, in the middle of the shop, were Midori and Shōtarō, two or three younger children by their side, all playing tiddlywinks with little sea-snail shells. Two, four, six, eight, ten… Shōtarō was counting out his winnings. Suddenly, Midori pricked up her ears. Is that a customer? she said, hearing footsteps on the gutter boards outside the shop. Really? asked Shōtarō, pausing his tally. I didn't hear anything. Maybe it's someone come to play? he said hopefully. The footsteps made it as far as the entrance to the shop, but then, suddenly, they stopped. There was silence.

II.

Boo! Shōtarō slid the door open and poked his head out. He could just make out the back of a figure walking under the eaves two or three houses away. Who is it? the others chorused. Tell them to come in! He slipped on Midori's rain clogs and darted out in spite of the deluge. It's him! he said, turning back to the group and pretending to shave his head. Fat chance of him coming back! He wouldn't come, even if you shouted for him, Midori…

You mean it was Nobu? she said. That nasty bonze? I can't stand him. I'll bet he came to buy himself a writing brush or something and ran off home the minute he heard us. He's just a mean, twisted, gap-toothed, stammering old creep. I hate him! If he had come in, I'd have teased him mercilessly. It's a pity he ran off, really. Give me those *geta*, I want to take a look! Midori recoiled as the rain dripped down on her from the eaves, but she could just make out the back of Nobuyuki's head under the gaslight four or five houses down. He was plodding along, hunched over, his gaze seemingly fixed on the ground. Midori just stood there, watching and watching and watching. What's the matter? Shōtarō asked, tapping her on the shoulder.

It's nothing, she replied listlessly, stepping back into the shop and counting out her shells. It's just that I really can't stand that boy. He goes around with that holier-than-thou look on his face, acting as though he'd never get into a fight. And all the while he's just sniggering up his sleeve. Don't you just hate him? My mother always says that plain-spoken folk have good hearts. Well, then, Nobu must have a wicked one with all that duplicity of his. Don't you think? At least he knows a thing or two, unlike that feckless good-for-nothing

Chōkichi, said Shōtarō, aping the way adults talked. So wise and yet so young! Midori laughed, poking him playfully in the cheek. You are funny, you know, acting all grown up! she added, seeing the earnest expression on the boy's face. I'll have you know that it won't be long before I *am* all grown up! And when I am, I'll get to wear a big overcoat just like the owner of the Kabata-ya. I've already got the gold pocket watch that grandmother saved for me! And then I'll have a ring made and start smoking cigarettes. Now, what shall I wear today? I'll think to myself. And I'll prefer leather sandals to wooden *geta*—and not just any old kind, but a good pair, with a three-ply heel and a strap made of brocade! I'll look *debonair*! Midori laughed. A shrimp like you? In an overcoat and triple heels?! Well, it's certainly a look—that is, if you don't mind looking like a bottle on stilts. Oh, come off it! I'll be all grown up by then, boasted Shōtarō, so I'm bound to be taller than I am now, aren't I! Well, I wouldn't hold my breath… Listen! Even the mice in the ceiling are even laughing at the idea. They were all of them, even the brush-maker's wife now, rolling about with laughter.

All, that is, except for Shōtarō. He alone wore a look of solemnity and rolled his eyes. You're always poking fun at me, Midori! But everyone grows up, don't they? What did I say that was so very funny? One day, I'll have a beautiful wife, and I'll take her walking with me. I'd only want her if she's pretty, though. I couldn't have a pockmarked one like the *sembei*-seller's wife, O-Fuku, or that one with the bulging forehead behind the counter at the firewood merchant's. If either of them came along, I wouldn't let them through the door! Give them *short shrift*, I would. No siree, it'd be thank you and goodnight from Shōtarō! His little tirade made the brush-maker's wife laugh. And yet, you still deign to patronize my little shop, dear? she said. How very kind of you! Haven't you noticed my pockmarks, then? Oh, but that's different! I'm talking about girls I'd marry. It doesn't matter if you're old, like you. Always the way, she sighed, humouring the boy good-naturedly.

Now let me think, she continued. The prettiest girls in the neighbourhood are O-Roku, in the flower shop, and Miss Kii at the fruiterer's. Oh, and then, of course, don't let's forget the prettiest one of all—why, the one who's sitting right beside you! Well, which is it to be? O-Roku of the lovely eyes? Or Miss Kii with her lovely singing voice? Hmm? Which one? Shōtarō's face blushed a deep scarlet. What's she on about? O-Roku's eyes and that Kii girl… I don't see what's so special about them, he said, shrinking from the light of the hanging lamp. Ah, so it must be Midori, then! the shop lady said, seeing how he recoiled. I'm right, aren't I? She had hit the nail on the head, but still Shōtarō answered, How should I know? In a temper, he turned to face the wall, where he started humming a little children's ditty, 'Round and Around the Waterwheel Goes', as he tapped out the rhythm on the wainscoting. Meanwhile, Midori and the others were getting ready for another game of tiddlywinks, her face a model of composure.

12.

He could always have taken another route when he went to visit his sister in Tamachi, but the shortcut—as it were—along the embankment led him past a certain little gate, where, if he peered in through the slats, he could catch a glimpse of the Kurama-stone lanterns, the elegant thatched fence and the rolled-up rattan blinds that hung along the veranda. Oh! how evocative that scene was! There, behind a glass-panelled *shōji*, her mother would sit, fingering her rosary like some latter-day Azechi's widow, while standing there beside her, tresses still flowing, like a young Murasaki, would be her daughter.* This grand edifice belonged to the owner of the Daikoku-ya.

For two days, the autumn rains had not let up, but the long winter under-kimono that Nobuyuki's sister had requested was ready, and, anxious that she should have it, her mother had asked the boy to deliver it. I hate to ask, what with this weather, but it's only a stone's throw from the school, and I just know your sister will be waiting for it! The meek child could not bring himself to say no. With a simple Yes, Mother!, he took the package under his arm, slipped on his sensible magnolia-wood *geta*, and tottered off, holding aloft an enormous black umbrella.

Turning at the corner by the moat, he picked his way along the narrow embankment as usual, but—what terrible

* In *The Tale of Genji*, the widow of Azechi no Dainagon renounces the world and becomes a nun after her husband's death.

luck!—as he reached the Daikoku-ya that day, a sudden gust of wind caught the top of his umbrella and blew with such violence that Nobuyuki thought he would be lifted into the air. Realizing the precarity of the situation, he planted his feet, bracing himself against the wind—but just then, of all things, the strap of his *geta* snapped clean off, presenting an even greater problem.

Tsk! What was he to do now? He propped his umbrella against the gate of the Daikoku-ya and stepped under the shelter of the awning to escape the rain. There, loath though he was, he tried to mend the broken strap. But this son of a bonze was unused to such work, and, no matter how he tried, he grew flustered and, oh, so impatient, exasperated that he could not even manage as simple a task as this. From his sleeve he extracted the draft of an essay he had composed for school on a piece of foolscap and immediately tore it into strips, which he then twisted to fashion a new strap of sorts. But just then, the cruel tempest struck again: the wind got up and blew his umbrella away. Curses! He reached out to stop it, but—what terrible luck!—as he did so, the package that had been resting in his lap went tumbling to the ground, and now the *furoshiki*—and presently his sleeves, too—were covered in mud.

The sight of somebody caught in the rain without an umbrella is pitiful enough, but to see them with a broken sandal into the bargain was too much. Midori gazed out through the glass of the *shōji*, wondering who this pathetic figure might be. Mother, should we give him something to fix it? she asked. She took a scrap of *yūzen* crêpe from the drawer of her sewing box, slipped on the pair of burnt-cedar *geta* she used for walking in the garden, and impatiently, before she even had time to open the Western-style umbrella she had seized from the veranda, set out for the gate, her feet carrying her swiftly across the stepping stones in the garden.

The moment Midori saw who it was, her face flushed red, and her heart began to beat so quickly and furiously that one might have wondered what terrible calamity had befallen her. She instinctively looked around to see whether anybody was watching, and then cautiously—but so very cautiously—approached the gate. Nobuyuki suddenly looked up and saw her. Speechless, he could feel cold perspiration dripping down under his arm. He was even tempted to kick off his remaining *geta* and flee in his bare feet.

Under ordinary circumstances, Midori would have pointed at Nobuyuki's plight and laughed heartily. Well, well, well, she might have said, quite the predicament, isn't it! She would have mocked him with every choice turn of phrase she could think of. After all, how dare he spoil their fun on the night of the festival! All because he had some grudge against Shōtarō! And having them beat up poor innocent Sangorō like that, while he sat in the background, pulling all the strings? Didn't he owe them an apology? Well, didn't he?! And had it not been on his authority that Chōkichi and the others had called her a whore? So what if she worked in the Yoshiwara? She didn't need anything from him—not one jot! She had her mother, her father, the owner of the

Daikoku-ya and her sister. What could she possibly want from that creep of a joss-merchant? He'd better take her name out of that sanctimonious mouth of his. If he had something to say about her or her line of work, then better to say it to her face than to whisper it behind her back. She was ready to show him, all right—any time he wanted. What about it, eh? She was ready to shake him by the sleeves and read him the riot act—and, if she had done, the bonze wouldn't have had a prayer. But instead, she just hid behind the slats, not daring to utter a word. Indecision rooted her to the spot. Her heart was pounding. This was not at all like her.

13.

Whenever he approached the Daikoku-ya, Nobuyuki was overcome with terror. He would always walk straight on, his eyes fixed forward. But that day, what with the ill-fated rain, the ill-fated wind and the ill-fated strap on his *geta*, he had no choice but to stop at the gate and fiddle around with those infernal scraps of paper. And, as if that weren't bad enough, just when he thought things couldn't get any worse, there were the footsteps coming down the garden path. It was as if somebody had thrown a bucket of iced water over his back. Even without turning to look, he knew that it was Midori herself. His quivering seemed to shake the colour from his face. Turning his back to her, he pretended to busy himself with the strap, but, even in his daze, he knew that, no matter how he tried, he would never be able to mend the shoe.

Standing there in the garden, Midori peered at Nobuyuki. What on earth is he trying to do with those ridiculous hands of his? she wondered. Making a strap out of paper?! Wonders will never cease! And is he trying to fix it in place with straw? Well, that's never going to hold. And, look! he's getting the cuffs of his *haori* all dirty. Doesn't he know they're trailing in the mud? Ugh, there goes his umbrella. Why didn't he think to fold it before standing it up? Everything about him is just so infuriating! she thought, but still, she didn't call out, Here, you can use this! or Why not try fixing it with this? Instead, she just stood there in silence, hidden, peeping at him through the gate, her poor sleeves getting sodden in the rain. Yet her mother, oblivious to all this, suddenly called out from the house: Midori! The iron's ready! What are you playing at in this rain? Come in at once, or you'll catch your death out there! Coming, Mother! Midori shouted back. It shamed her to know that Nobuyuki would have heard that voice. Her heart was racing and she felt light-headed. She hesitated. She could hardly open the gate now, but as she stood there beside it, she couldn't just leave the poor wretch fumbling around. Eventually, without a word, she threw the scrap of cloth she had been clutching through the slats of the gate. But Nobuyuki pretended not to see it. Oh, he was just as mean-spirited as ever! Tears of bitterness and resentment welled now in Midori's eyes. Why did he have to be so spiteful? What was it that he had against her? There were so many things she wanted to say to him, but this dizzying flood of thoughts and emotions prevented her from doing so. It was so overwhelming that she felt sick. And still her mother kept calling her. How wretched she felt! And yet there was nothing for it. Placing one foot in front of the other, she started back towards the house. But what on earth was she thinking, feeling like that? She ought to be ashamed of herself… Now Nobuyuki heard her go stomping off across the garden stones, but when he turned around it was too late. Forlorn, he spotted the scrap of crimson fabric soaked through in the rain, its lovely pattern of maple leaves seemingly scattered at his feet. It ought to have been a comforting sight, and, in a curious way, seeing it did move him. But still, the boy just kept staring at it vacantly, not daring to reach down and pick it up.

Having resigned himself by now to his own clumsiness, Nobuyuki removed the tassel from his *haori*, twisted it around and fashioned it into a makeshift strap. I suppose it'll have to do, he thought, as he tried it out. Not only was it difficult to walk in, but he wondered whether this abomination would hold out all the way to Tamachi. It was a concern. Still, what alternative was there? he thought, getting to his feet. He replaced the *furoshiki* under his arm and had taken only two steps away from the gate when he paused, the maple leaves still lingering in his mind's eye. He looked back, loath to leave them there… What's the matter, Nobu? Broke your strap? Oh dear. Whose could the voice be? Well, you've made a right pig's ear of that, haven't you!

Nobuyuki turned around and was surprised to see Chōkichi standing there. Dressed as he was with a fine striped-cotton kimono over his *yukata*, and with a persimmon *obi* fixed, as usual, low around his waist, the young ruffian looked as though had just come from the Yoshiwara. His new winter coat had a luxurious collar of heavy black silk, and the umbrella he was carrying was emblazoned with the name of one of the houses. It was clear to see, moreover, that the gleaming lacquered toe-caps he wore on his tall rain clogs had been put on newly that morning. Truly, he cut a rather dashing figure.

It snapped and I couldn't think how to mend it, Nobu said feebly. I'm really no good at that sort of thing. I'll say! There's no way you'll be able to walk in those. Here, take mine. Just be sure not to break them! But then what will you do? Don't you worry about me, I'm used it. I'll just go back like this, he said, hastily hitching up the hem of his kimono just below the knee. I prefer walking like this anyway, he added, taking off his *geta*. You're going to go barefoot?! I can't let you do that… It's fine, seriously. Like I say, I'm used to it. But you, on the other hand—your dainty feet will get all cut up on the gravel. Hurry up, you'd best just put them on, he said, arranging them nicely for Nobuyuki. Though some might have despised him, shunning him as though he were the god of pestilence, there was, oddly enough, really something quite sweet about the boy's gentle way and those expressive eyebrows he had. Here, I'll take yours, he offered. You won't mind if I leave them by the back door, will you? Come on, let's swap. His good deed done, he picked up the broken *geta* and said, Go on, then,

I'll see you later at school. Parting then with this promise, Chōkichi headed home, while Nobuyuki set off for his sister's—the blushing *yūzen*, tinged with regret, left abandoned at the foot of the slatted gate.

14.

That year, there were no fewer than three Days of the Rooster, and, though the middle one had been a washout, yet the two on either side of it fell on days when the weather was fine, sending terrific crowds flocking to the Ōtori Shrine. Under this pretext, hordes of young men and women practically stormed the rear gate of the Yoshiwara, trying to get in. So thunderous was the commotion, filled as it was with cries and laughter, that it threatened to shatter the very Pillars of Heaven and smite the rope from which the Earth itself hangs. The main thoroughfare through the quarter suddenly seemed to have changed direction. All around, the drawbridges had been lowered, and now crowds of pilgrims flooded in, all pushing and shoving, parting the waves of people as though they were river taxis. Make way! Coming through! From the twittering of the girls in the lowly brothels that line the embankment, to the great warblers that nest in the lofty heights of those grand houses, who could ever forget the song, the music, the excitement that filled the air? Because of the festival, Shōtarō had been given the day off from making his rounds of collections. He first went to visit Sangorō at his sweet-potato stall, before calling on Donkey, who was selling that sweet adzuki-bean porridge with *dango* he was not overly fond of. Well? Turning a profit? he asked. Shōtarō! Boy, am I glad to see you! I've just had to put some more adzuki beans on to cook. We've run out! What am I going to sell in the meantime? I don't want to turn away paying customers! But I don't know what to do… Scrape down the edges of the pot, you ass! Don't let that go to waste! Just mix in a bit of water and sugar to sweeten it and you'll have enough for ten, maybe twenty portions. Everybody does it! You certainly won't be the only stall here… Besides, is anybody really going to notice the quality with all this going on around? Go on, get to it! Shōtarō said, reaching for the sugar bowl himself. Gosh! said Donkey's one-eyed mother, turning to the boy with a look of astonishment. You really do have the makings of a merchant. What a frightfully clever lad you are! Oh, it's nothing, really. I spotted some ugly old blowhard doing the same in the alley just now. It's not as if I invented it, he said, looking back over his shoulder. By the way, you haven't seen Midori, have you? I've been looking for her all morning, but I just can't find her. She wasn't at the paper shop either. Maybe she's gone to the Yoshiwara… What's that? You're looking for Midori? I saw her go past not long ago. She was heading across the Ageya-machi drawbridge into the quarter. Oh, you should have seen her, Shōtarō! Had her hair all done up in a *shimada* like this, so she did! said Donkey, trying to describe the elegant coiffeur with his ungainly hands. Bea-utiful, she looked! He wiped his nose. I bet she was even prettier than her big sister! said Shōtarō. Too bad she'll end up an *oiran* like her, though.* He looked at his feet. So what if she does? Is that really so bad? Besides, I'm going to start working at the novelty shop next year—with all the money I'll make there, I'll have enough to go and buy her out! he said, revealing his naïveté. Ha! If you try anything like that, she's bound to give you the cold shoulder. Why?! What makes you say that? Because she can, that's why! Blushing ever so slightly, the boy laughed. Well, I'm off for a wander, he said. I'll be back later. And with that, he strutted off out the gate.

> As she grows, she is tended
> like a butterfly, a flower…

There was an odd quaver in his voice as he sang the popular refrain.

> … but none knows better than she now
> the stings of toil and of care.

As he repeated the lyrics to himself, his leather-soled *geta* struck out their usual rhythms, drowned by the merry fray into which this little figure now vanished.

Borne by the jostling crowd, he found himself in a corner of the Yoshiwara, and it was there he spotted her coming towards him, chatting away to a lady attendant from one of the houses. There could be no doubting it. Here was

* That is, a high-ranking courtesan.

Midori of the Daikoku-ya. And she was just as Donkey said she would be, with the magnificent *shimada* of an innocent young maiden, however incongruous that might have seemed in these surroundings. Her hair was adorned, moreover, with a tortoiseshell comb, tie-dyed bows and ribbons, and an ornamental hairpin with flower tassels that glinted in the sunlight. Arrayed there in such singularly gay colours, she might have been taken for a Kyoto doll. Shōtarō was speechless. He didn't dare to go and hug her as he usually would; instead, he just stood there, rooted to the spot, staring at her. Well, if it isn't Shōtarō! Midori hurried over to him. O-Tsuma, she said, turning to her companion, if you've got some shopping to do, why don't we part ways here? I'll have this young swain see me home… Oh, so that's how it is! I'm surplus to requirement now, am I? O-Tsuma said, laughing as she bowed. Very nice, I'm sure! I'll be off to do some shopping in Kyōmachi in that case. And with that, she darted off down a narrow alley between two rows of shops. Shōtarō tugged at Midori's sleeve. It suits you, he said. When did you have your hair done? This morning? Yesterday? Why didn't you come and show me? He pouted, a little hurt. But Midori was sullen and taciturn. They did it for me this morning in my sister's room. I hate it, she said. But I didn't have much choice in the matter. She lowered her gaze to the ground, embarrassed to be seen.

15.

So terribly shy and reserved was she that the praise of others sounded to her like ridicule. When others turned to admire her charming *shimada*, she mistook their delight for mockery. I think I'll go home, Shōtarō. Why? I thought you'd want to enjoy yourself today. You didn't get a telling-off, did you? Or have a fight with your sister? His questions were so boyish and naïve, but in response Midori only blushed. As they passed the *dango* stall, Donkey called out, My, my, what a fine and handsome pair you make! But his exaggerated words only made Midori want to cry. Her face dropped. I can't walk with you any more, Shōtarō! Abandoning him there, she ran off.

She had promised Shōtarō that she would accompany him to the shrine, and yet there she was, hurrying away in the opposite direction. Why do you want to go home? I thought we were going to the Ōtori together, he whined. That isn't fair! Hoping to shake him off, she just carried on without a word to him. In the dark and at a loss to explain her actions, he ran after her, clutching at her sleeve. He looked at her beseechingly. She blushed. It's nothing, she said.

When Midori slipped through the gate to her home, Shōtarō, who had been going there to play for some time already and thus felt no need to stand on ceremony, followed her in directly and went up to the veranda. Oh, Shōtarō! the girl's mother said, seeing him. I'm so pleased you're here. Midori's been in such a foul temper all morning. We just don't what to do with her! She's all yours... Has anything happened?

Shōtarō enquired solemnly, mustering all the grown-up tone he could. No, the girl's mother replied, a mysterious smile upon her lips. Just give her some time. She's so spoilt, that girl! I suppose Madam's been quarrelling with her friends as well, has she? She really is the limit sometimes! Her mother turned to look at her, but Midori had already gone into the small parlour. There, having discarded her *obi* and jacket on the floor, she had laid out a futon and, without a word, crawled under the quilt, lying face down.

Shōtarō approached her warily. What's the matter, Midori? Are you not feeling well? Tell me, won't you? What on earth's going on? Concerned for her, he knelt by her side, his hands in his lap, careful not to draw too near. But still Midori said nothing as she sobbed quietly into her sleeves. He could see that her fringe, too short to have tied up, was damp, plainly from all the tears. But what words could he, a mere child, offer her by way of comfort? He was at a loss entirely. Won't you please tell me what it is? I haven't done anything to upset you, so why are you angry with me? As he peered at her, he felt utterly bewildered. Midori dried her eyes. It isn't you, Shōtarō, she said.

But what, then? The question was hard to answer. All sorts of things, really. Sad things, painful things. Things about which she was too embarrassed to talk, about which she had no one to confide in. Without uttering a word, her cheeks flushed crimson. Although she could not put her finger on it, yet it was making her feel increasingly uneasy. Where had they come from, all these thoughts and emotions that had never crossed her mind until that day? She felt an indescribable sense of shame. Oh, if only she could spend her days and nights locked away in some darkened room, where nobody would see or talk to her! That way, even if something awful happened, she wouldn't have to worry so much about what others thought. If only she could just go on playing house for ever, with her dolls for companions, how happy she would surely be. Oh, I hate it, I hate it! she thought. I don't want to be a grown-up! Must I really age like this? What I'd give to go back a year, ten months, seven months, even! Her thoughts were already those of an old woman. By now, she had quite forgotten that Shōtarō was there. Hearing him speak, she wanted nothing more than to drive him away. Go home, Shōtarō! For the love of Heaven, I beg you, go home! I'll simply die if you stay here any longer! All this talk of yours is giving me a headache and making me dizzy. I don't want to see anyone! Please, won't you just go home! Such heartlessness was entirely out of character for her. Struggling to understand the reasons for it, Shōtarō felt as though he were lost amid a cloud of smoke. You shouldn't go saying things like that, Midori! You know, you're really acting strange today. I suppose there must be something very wrong with you. He already regretted saying it. Though his words had been measured, faint-hearted tears were now welling in his eyes. But what kind of sympathy could he expect now? Go home! Just go home, will you! What are you waiting for? I'm through with you! I hate you, Shōtarō! There was venom in her words. Well, if that's how you feel, I will go!

So sorry to have bothered you! He shot to his feet. Then, without even saying goodbye to Midori's mother, who had gone off to check on the bath she was running, he rushed out through the garden.

16.

Like an arrow, Shōtarō shot through the crowds of revellers, ducking and diving all the way to the paper shop, where he came tearing in to find Sangorō, his stall having sold out some while ago and the jangling profits burning a hole in the pocket of his apron. He was playing the benevolent older brother, telling the others to buy whatever they liked—Anything, anything at all!—and it was amid this general merriment that Shōtarō happened upon the scene. Ah, Shōtarō! I've been looking for you! I made a real killing today! Let me treat you to something... Don't be absurd! Since when do *you* treat *me*? Look at yourself, throwing it around like that. Just shut up, will you, and knock it off. I'm in no mood for it. Sangorō had never heard his friend utter such fierce words before. What's all this? Did you get into a scrape? he said, shoving a half-eaten *anpan* into his pocket. Who's got you so riled up? That bonze from Ryūge Temple? Chōkichi? Where was it? In the quarter? Outside the shrine? If there's going to be another fight, it won't be like last time, I can tell you that! If we know they're coming for us, we can't lose. I'm ready for them, Shōtarō! Let me at them! Come on, we can't duck out now! Sangorō was champing at the bit, but Shōtarō reined him in. Whoa! Hold your horses! There's not going to be any fight. Still finding it hard to speak, he bit his tongue. But the way you came storming in here! I was sure you were looking for trouble! But, Shōtarō, listen: if we don't get them tonight, we won't get another chance. Chōkichi's losing his right arm... What do you mean, losing his right arm? You haven't heard, then? I only just found out about it myself. Pa was talking to the abbot's wife, and she told him that Nobu's being sent off to some priest school any day now. Once he puts on those robes, he'll be out of reach, unable to take a swing at anyone. And all because of those flimsy long sleeves he'll have. I guess he'd never be able to roll them up, eh? Still, it means that next year the high street *and* the back streets will be all yours! Give over, Shōtarō shot back. Two *sen* are all it would take for them to switch sides and join Chōkichi. I could have a hundred lads like you and it still wouldn't make any difference. Join them if you like. Or not. What do I care? I don't need anyone else. What I really wanted was to take on Nobu myself, but there's not much I can do about it if the coward's going to run away. Why's he going off so soon, anyway? I'd heard he wasn't going until after he finished school next year... For all his tutting, though, he didn't really care all that much about Nobuyuki; it was Midori's behaviour that kept preying on his mind, preventing him from singing his usual songs. The immense crowds outside only made him feel lonelier still. What did they have to be so happy about? At dusk, while the lamps were being lit, he lay down on the shop floor. The day had been a strange one.

*

From that day on, Midori was a changed person. She would still go to visit her sister in the Yoshiwara whenever the need took her, but no longer did she go out to play in the neighbourhood. Missing her company, the girl's friends would call to invite her out, but now she just brushed them off with empty promises. I'll be right there! Her affections for Shōtarō, moreover, with whom she had once been the greatest of friends, had cooled. It was rare now to see that old vivaciousness of hers, the one that had made her blush as she danced and played in the paper shop. People grew suspicious. Perhaps she was ill? some even suggested. But Midori's mother merely smiled and said, She'll be right as rain again in no time! She's just having a bit of a rest now. Indeed, to those who knew no better, it was all something of a mystery. For every person who now praised her ladylike restraint, there was another who mourned the passing of that singularly pert child. All of a sudden, the high street took on a bleak, washed-out aspect, as if all the lights in it had been put out. Shōtarō's beautiful singing voice was rarely heard now. Only at night would you see him on his rounds, lantern in hand, picking his way along the embankment. His silhouette looked cold, somehow. The only thing that never changed was Sangorō's laughter, which rang out beside him on occasion.

Rumours that Nobuyuki would soon take the cloth failed to reach Midori. Cloistered herself, she now shut away her old nature, too. She had changed so very much lately that she scarcely even recognized herself. Every little thing embarrassed her now. But one frosty morning, somebody came and slipped a paper narcissus through the slats of the garden gate. Although she had no way of knowing who was responsible for it, the girl was, unaccountably, quite taken with it. She placed the flower in a small vase, which she then stood on set of staggered shelves, and there she admired its platonic, solitary beauty. Later that same day, quite by chance, she heard that Nobuyuki would be entering a seminary, and that tomorrow he would don his priestly robes.

TROUBLED WATERS

(Nigorie)

1.

WELL, LOOK WHO IT IS! Kimura-san, Shin-san, over here! You're always saying you'll call, but then you never do. You were hoping to sneak past on your way to the Two Leaves again without stopping to say hello, weren't you? Just you wait… Next time I'll come over there and drag you back here myself! Do be sure to drop in on your way back—if you really are going to the bathhouse, that is. The two of you are such fibbers that I never quite know what to believe… The two men in *geta* were seemingly regular patrons of this establishment, but rather than get angry when the woman's haranguing from her spot in front of the place stopped them in their tracks, they instead merely carried on, fobbing her off with promises. (Later, later!) The woman tutted as she watched them go. Later, my foot! she muttered to herself as she stepped back inside. Honestly, it's always the way once they're married… Oh, how you do go on, O-Taka! said one of the other girls, trying to calm her. You really oughtn't to worry so much. What is it they say? The embers of love always blaze anew? Just wait a little, or cast a charm if you're so terribly anxious. But I don't have the knack for it like O-Riki does! I'd hate to let even one of them get away... And my luck's so poor that I can't well rely on charms or anything like that. I'm probably going to be left on the door again tonight. Oh, the shame of it! And it's such a bore, too. With that, she sat down in front of the place in a fit of pique, kicking at the ground with the heels of her *koma-geta*. She was a woman in her late twenties, maybe thirty, even, with eyebrows plucked bare and hairline neatly outlined, her face caked in white powder and her lips painted blood-red, like those of a hound that had just eaten a man. The woman they called O-Riki was slender and of average height. Her freshly washed hair had been done up in a large *shimada*-style chignon and tied neatly in place with a length of new straw. As for make-up, she wore white powder at the nape of her neck, but its brilliance paled next to the beautiful lustre of her own skin, which she left exposed down to her breast. Her manners were exceedingly lax, and she would sit unconventionally, with one knee raised, puffing away on her long *kiseru*. (She was lucky there was nobody there to give her a telling-off.) A single glance was enough to know how she earned her living. The pattern of her *yukata* was bold and daring—a hallmark of the profession—and her *obi* was a mixture of black satin and some kind of cheaper imitation fabric, with garish scarlet stitching on the reverse. Scratching under her topknot with a nickel-silver hairpin, O-Taka turned to O-Riki, as if just remembering something. Did you post that letter? she asked. Indeed I did, replied O-Riki listlessly. But he won't come. I was just being polite. She laughed. Oh, give over! Is it really just being polite to use up two rolls of letter paper and affix two stamps? And anyway, wasn't he that regular from Akasaka? Do you really want to let things end like that over a little tiff? Besides, can you really afford to? It's up to you, of course, but if you'll take my advice, I think you could stand to make a little more effort with him. One of these days, your luck will run out, you know! How kind of you to say… I'll bear that in mind—but, truth be told, I'm not overly keen on the chap. It's over. So, I'd drop it if I were you. You really are the limit! laughed O-Taka, reaching for an *uchiwa* to cool her feet. You may get away with that sort of thing now, acting all grand like that, but it won't last for ever, you know. Just you wait and see. Once upon a time, I had men queuing out the door every evening. Said I was a real flower of a girl, so they did…

The establishment was a two-storey double-fronted affair with lanterns hanging from the eaves. Placed by the entrance were little dishes piled generously with salt to bring in good luck, and, on the shelves behind the bar, one could see a great quantity of bottles (whether empty or otherwise, who could say?), each with a label designating a famous brand of sake. Every now and then, the clatter of the charcoal brazier being stoked could be heard coming from the kitchen. The proprietress herself prepared simple fare such as stew and *chawanmushi*, although the signboard hanging outside gave the distinct impression that this was a restaurant of some standing. Whatever would they tell the unsuspecting customer who stopped there by chance and actually ordered a meal? That they had suddenly run out of everything? That this restaurant catered only to men? Fortunately, people always seemed to discern the true nature of the place, and so even the most rustic types refrained from coming in and ordering snacks and grilled fish. The most popular dish on the house's bill of fare, however, was O-Riki. Though she was the youngest of the girls, she had a curious knack for drawing in punters. She was not especially friendly towards them, nor did she bother with the customary pleasantries; in fact, her egotism and wilfulness were of the utmost degree. She was a little too proud of her looks, whispered the other girls behind her back, and too pert—but, as soon as you got to know her, you discovered (and quite unexpectedly) that there was a sweet side to her as well; even women found themselves drawn to her. There were those who supposed the blithe look on her face to be a mark of her true character. And indeed, the heart is not something that can easily be hidden… There was not a man who set foot in the new quarter without having heard of O-Riki of the Chrysanthemum Well. But then, we might as well be speaking of the Chrysanthemum Well of O-Riki, for such had been the recent success of this rare find. Indeed, it was for O-Riki that all the lanterns of the new quarter burned. Her employers ought to count their blessings, envious neighbours had begun to say. I shouldn't be surprised if they even placed the girl herself up on the family altar…

Taking advantage of a lull in footfall outside, O-Taka said: It's none of my business, I know, O-Riki, but honestly, if I were in your shoes… It's Genshichi I feel sorry for. I know he's on his uppers these days, and he's not exactly what one might call a first-rate client, but when the two of you were so sweet on each other... Yes, he's a lot older than you. Yes, he's got a wife and a child. Be that as it may. But is that any reason to go and break things off with him? If I were you, I'd have him back. Now, my men—they're another lot altogether. No sooner do I fall for these ne'er-do-wells than they run a mile. What can I say? I've no choice but to give them up and go looking for someone new. But, oh no, not you. Why, the solution's obvious! All you have to do is to convince Genshichi to get a divorce. Your trouble is that you're too proud to settle for someone like him. But all the same, I don't see the harm in asking to see him. A few words are all it would take. The messenger from the Mikawa-ya will be along any moment now. Why not send the boy with a note? You're no ingénue, after all—there's no sense in being so coy. What you need is to be decisive. Just write the letter and see what comes of it. How I do pity poor Genshichi...

O-Riki just looked down and said nothing to this, seemingly engrossed in the cleaning of her *kiseru*. Having wiped the gooseneck crook of the pipe clean, she drew on it once, tapped it, and filled it afresh with tobacco. Then she lit it and handed it to O-Taka, saying, Watch what you say out here... Somebody might overhear and get the wrong impression. We wouldn't want people thinking that O-Riki of the Chrysanthemum Well has a workman for a lover, now, would we? The whole thing is a figment of your imagination, a dream long forgotten. Why, I can hardly even remember his name nowadays. You're never to speak of him again, do you hear me? As she said all this, O-Riki stood up and went over to the door. A group of students whom she recognized by the way their *obi* were tied was passing by. Yoo-hoo! Ishikawa-san! Muraoka-san! she called to them. You haven't forgotten me and my humble establishment, have you? Perish the thought! a voice replied. How could we ever resist the voice of such a temptress?! And so, the students all piled inside, filling the hallway with the rumble of footsteps and calls of Hey, bring us some sake, will you? and What snacks do you have? Before long, the lively strains of a *shamisen* could be heard to the accompaniment of heavy footfall: the dancing and revelry had begun in earnest.

2.

Amid the tedium of a rainy day, a man in his thirties wearing an elegant bowler hat came strolling idly by the Chrysanthemum Well. Spotting him, O-Riki dashed out, knowing just how unlikely it was that she would manage to snare another client in such a downpour. I'm not letting you get away! she cried petulantly, clinging to his sleeves. (Such daring was the privilege of her beauty.) She then led this singularly impressive man inside and showed him to a little private room upstairs, where amid an intimate hush they fell into conversation, apparently without the need of any *shamisen* to entertain them. The gentleman enquired her name and age and where she came from. Was she perchance the daughter of a samurai? I am bound to silence… came her reply. A commoner, then? Is that what you think? A noblewoman? he asked at last, laughing. If it pleases you… How would you like to be served by a lady-in-waiting? she said, filling his sake cup to the brim. Some lady-in-waiting! he exclaimed, watching the offhand way she poured. Wherever did you learn manners like that? Is that the Ogasawara School?* It's the O-Riki School, she replied, and I can assure you, it's quite the correct etiquette around here. Sometimes we even make the *tatami* mats drink, and on occasion we serve sake in the lids of large bowls and make our patrons drink them down in a single draught. We also make it a point of honour not to serve people we don't like. Such is our code of conduct. Her manner was entirely relaxed, which seemed only to intrigue the gentleman all the more. Tell me about yourself, he said. You must have quite a story. I can't imagine yours to have been any conventional upbringing. Well, am I right? See for yourself! I don't have any horns growing out of my temples. And I haven't grown any scales yet, either, she said, chuckling. Oh, I'm not letting you get away that easily, said the gentleman. Tell me the truth. And if you can't tell me your past, then tell me your dreams. He was most insistent. That's just it, you see, she said. If I were to tell you, I dare say you'd be scandalized… I have ambition in spades—enough to rival Ōtomo no Kuronushi,

* With its origins in the Kamakura period, the Ogasawara School is one of Japan's oldest and most famous schools of etiquette, having originally set down codes of conduct for the samurai class.

who desired the heavens and the earth itself. She laughed at herself. Oh, you are the limit! Stop fooling around for a moment and be serious, said the man. Even if you do spend your days and nights spinning all manner of tall tales, there must be a grain of truth mixed in there somewhere. Did you lose your husband? Or are you doing this all for the sake of your parents? As the gentleman's questions became more earnest, a sense of melancholy descended over O-Riki. I am only human, after all, she said, and there are matters that lance my heart. My parents died while I was still young, and now I have only myself to rely on. Of course there have been men who, in spite of my profession, would have been only too pleased to have me as their wedded wife, but never to this day have I been married. I was brought up in such abject poverty that I'll probably live out the remainder of my days doing this. She offered these words casually, but behind this façade of nonchalance, she was teeming with emotion, no longer even trying to seduce him. I shouldn't imagine that an impoverished upbringing would be any impediment to finding a husband. Not least for a pretty thing like you. Who knows! One day, you could suddenly find yourself marrying into a family of rank and means. Or perhaps you don't want to be treated like a lady and would prefer to take up with some young ruffian downtown? You're not far off the mark. I never much care for the ones who are sweet on me, and none of the ones I go in for ever seems to fall for me. You must think me very fickle, but that's how it is, I'm afraid… Oh, you mustn't talk like that! I should have thought you'd have a great many young gallants chasing after you. Why, wasn't one of the other girls only just saying there was a man at the door looking for you? My, my, a girl like you must have a great deal of intrigue to keep her busy! You really are a nosey one, aren't you? But it's true, I have a raft of suitors. And all those love letters we exchange aren't worth the paper they're written on. Why, if you asked me to write to you, I'd write whatever tender words you wanted—I'd pledge myself to you or give you my solemn oath… But what men seem to want most of all from women like me are promises of marriage. And don't think we're the ones who go breaking them. Before I even have the chance, it's the men who'll break it off for—fear of their wives, if they already have one, or else their parents. What cowards men are! If a man turns his back on me, I'm not going to go chasing after him, clutching at his sleeves. Let him be, I tell myself, and that's the end of that… No, no matter how many men have come my way, there hasn't been one to whom I'd entrust my life, said O-Riki despondently. Truly, the man thought, she did seem to be all alone in the world. But enough of all that! she said suddenly. Let's not dwell on those things. You're here to have a good time, after all! How I do hate melancholy… Come, let's really cut loose! With that, she clapped her hands to summon the other girls. You've been awfully quiet today, O-Riki! said one of the ladies who came—she was in her thirties, and her face was heavily made up. Say, won't you tell me what her boyfriend's name is? the gentleman asked all of a sudden. What? Oh, she hasn't even told me that herself! You mustn't go telling fibs, otherwise you won't be able to pay your respects to Lord Enma during the Festival of the Dead, the gentleman teased, laughing. Be that as it may, you and I have only just met. Isn't it a little too soon to go revealing secrets? And besides, I was just about to ask you myself. Ask me what? Why, your name of course! You are O-Riki's boyfriend, aren't you? What a flirt! You'll only make her cross... Their banter had done a great deal to liven up the atmosphere. Shall I try to divine what line of work you're in? O-Taka asked the gentleman. Be my guest, he replied, offering her his palm. No, I won't be needing that. I'm going to read it in your features, O-Taka said calmly, peering into the man's face. Enough, dear girl! All this stocktaking is making me nervous. I may not look it, but I'm really a government official. You're lying, said O-Taka. What sort of official goes out jaunting in the pleasure quarter right in the middle of the week? What do you suppose our esteemed guest does for a living, O-Riki? Well, you may rest assured that your esteemed guest is no humbug, the gentleman said. How about a prize for whoever gets it right? he added, plucking a wallet from the breast of his kimono. O-Riki laughed. You ought to mind your manners, O-Taka, she said. Why, this gentleman is clearly a man of rank, an aristocrat come to take his pleasures incognito. Why should you suppose he has a profession at all, when so clearly he hasn't one. She seized the wallet, which the gentleman had set down on the floor cushion. Why don't you let me handle this? I'll see to it that everybody gets what they deserve, she said, playing the grand courtesan and removing the money before the gentleman even had a chance to answer. Yet the latter merely leant back against the pillar, taking in the scene. I'll leave it in your capable hands, he said. Truly, this was a magnanimous man.

Enough, O-Riki! You'll go too far, said O-Taka, seemingly taken aback by the girl's audacity. Oh, but the gentleman doesn't mind. Here's yours… and here's some for you… and here, take this large one and settle the bill at the front desk, then you can distribute what's left among the others. You'd better thank the gentleman for his kindness, she said, practically making it rain down money. This act was in fact one of her specialities, however, and so, being quite used to it, O-Taka simply and without much hesitation asked, Are you sure this all right, sir? before thanking him cursorily and snatching the money away. The gentleman laughed as he watched her go off. For a maid not yet twenty, she seems a little long in the tooth, he said. What a horrid thing to say! said O-Riki, getting up and opening the *shōji*. Leaning on the balustrade, she tapped her forehead to alleviate the headache she could feel coming on. And what about you? the gentleman asked. Don't you want any money? Not money, no, but there is one thing I'd like, she said, plucking the gentleman's business card from the folds of his *obi* and holding it out to him in mock entreaty. If I could just have this? she pleaded. Now how did you get that? I wonder, the gentleman said. You must give me your photo in return. If you come back next Saturday, we can have one taken of us together. As the gentleman got ready to leave, O-Riki did not try to detain him. I really must apologize for my behaviour today, she said, standing behind him and helping him on with his *haori*. I do hope you'll come and visit us again. You can spare me the empty oaths and apologies, he said, chuckling. And with that, he got briskly to his feet and began making his way downstairs, O-Riki hot on his heels and carrying his hat. You'll have to come another ninety-nine nights to see whether they were empty or not,* she said. O-Riki of the Chrysanthemum Well is not your average woman. You may just find that I surprise you... Hearing that the gentleman was leaving, the other girls came rushing out, along with the proprietress of the establishment, who left her post at the front desk. They thanked him profusely, and, when it was announced that the rickshaw he had ordered was ready and waiting, they all bundled out to see him off. Please visit us again! they chorused, this extravagant hospitality the afterglow of his largesse. Then, when the gentleman was finally gone, the girls all piled a mountain of thanks on O-Riki, their very own guardian deity.

3·

The gentleman's name was Yūki Tomonosuke. Although he called himself a libertine, yet he was not entirely devoid of substance. Unburdened as he was by work or cares (and also

---

* A reference to the Heian-period poet Ono no Komachi (*c.*825–*c.*900), who famously demanded that the nobleman Fukakusa no Shōshō court her for one hundred nights before she would become his lover, but he died on the ninety-ninth night.

by any wife or children), he was at that ideal stage in life to indulge in the pursuit of pleasure. Perhaps this was why, ever since that day, he had taken to visiting the Chrysanthemum Well two or three times a week. O-Riki, too, had in some curious way begun to grow fond of the man, and, if ever he did not visit for three days or more, she would now dispatch letters immediately. In their envy, the other girls were given to teasing her about this. How happy you must be, O-Riki! one might intone. A man as handsome and generous as he is sure to go far in life—and, when he does, he'll ask you to be his wife, so you'd better start being a little more careful. From now on, there'll be no more showing your legs in public or guzzling down sake from tea bowls, lest such uncouthness mar your chances. Another might sneer: What will poor Genshichi think when he hears about all this? Why, he'll be wild with jealousy. But O-Riki would simply answer: That reminds me... I'm going to see about having that road outside repaired. You know, it's just too embarrassing when Tomonosuke comes by carriage—the way those gutter boards rattle, it's practically impossible for anyone to pull up there. You lot will have to mend your ways a little, too, otherwise I'll no longer let you wait on him. Her directness was wont to provoke the girls' ire. Careful, O-Riki, they now cautioned her. With a vicious tongue like that, nobody's going to be asking you to be his wife. In fact, I've a good mind to tell Yūki-san what you're really like next time he visits, and then we'll see whether you're so bold. No sooner had she uttered these words than the man himself suddenly appeared. The girls threw themselves at him and launched into a diatribe against O-Riki. You should hear the way she speaks! She won't condescend to take our advice! You've got to give her a talking-to! And another thing, all that drinking can't be good for her... Yūki's face grew stern. You really oughtn't to drink so much, O-Riki, he chastened her. Oh, not you as well! said O-Riki. Can't you see that if it weren't for a drop or two of sake, I'd find this work so utterly unbearable? Besides, if I gave up drinking, this entire establishment would be as solemn as a Buddhist temple. Try putting yourself in my position! Yes, quite, quite... was all the reply that Yūki could muster.

One moonlit night, while O-Riki and Yūki were in their quiet nook upstairs as usual, a party of factory workers took a room on the ground floor and began to make a terrible din, singing and dancing, striking their empty rice bowls like tambourines, and generally carrying on with the other girls in the house. Seeming quite content, Yūki lay sprawled out on the floor, but when he tried to strike up a conversation with O-Riki, she gave only vague and distracted answers. All this racket seemed to be getting on her nerves. What's the matter? he asked. Do you have another headache coming on? Not a headache, no, she replied, but something else she got attacks of now and then. Attacks of what? Irritability? No. Women's troubles? No. What, then? he asked. She really couldn't say. Not to others, maybe, but you can certainly tell me. Come on, out with it! There was nothing wrong with her *per se*. She just got like that sometimes. It was all in her head. You really are impossible at times, you know. All these secrets of yours! Changing the subject, he asked her to tell him about her father, but she simply replied, I really couldn't say. She repeated the same answer again when he enquired about her mother, and yet again when he asked about her background. Make it up, then! Lie to me if you really must! But say something at least. Most women would jump at the chance to share their woes. And why shouldn't you tell me, after all? It's not as though we've only just met. Anyway, even if you refuse to tell me what it is, I can see that something's bothering you. Why, it's so obvious that even a blind man could see it! You needn't tell me, of course, but I'd like to know all the same. After all, what difference would it make? So, this *affliction* of yours… Oh, will these questions never cease?! If I told you, you'd see only too well how very tedious all this is, said O-Riki, even more distractedly.

Just then, one of the girls appeared from downstairs, bearing a tray of drinks. She whispered in O-Riki's ear that there was somebody at the door for her. No, I'd rather not, O-Riki said. Send him away. Tell him I'm entertaining this evening and that I've already had too much to drink. Even if I were to go down and see him, I wouldn't be much company. What a nuisance that man is, she added, with a scowl. That's really your answer? It is, said O-Riki, playing with the *shamisen* plectrum in her lap. Wearing a look of puzzlement, the girl stood up and left. Yūki, who had been following every word of this exchange, laughed as he watched her go. Don't demur on my account, he said. By all means, go down and see him. You needn't stand on ceremony with me. Besides, to turn your boyfriend away just like that would be too cruel. Go down and see him, I mean it. Or, better yet, why not invite him up here, and I'll just sit quietly in the corner? I promise not to cramp your style. All jokes aside, there really is no hiding from you, Yūki-san, is there? I suppose I might as well confess everything. The man downstairs is an old client of mine, by the name of Genshichi. He once had a thriving local business; he was a dealer of bedding, but now he's practically unrecognizable! A pauper, fallen on hard times, he's been reduced to living like a snail in some tiny house behind a greengrocer's. He's married and has a child. Really, he's much too old now to be visiting someone like me, but I can never seem to shake him off. He still manages to find various pretexts to call on me every so often. That's the man who's downstairs right now. I don't want to start having him turned away, but if I were to go down and see him now, there'd be no end of it. It really would be better if he just went home—no words, no fuss—even if it meant his resenting me. Let him think I'm a devil or a serpent: I'm already inured to it. Having said her piece, she placed the plectrum on the *tatami* mat and craned her neck so that she could see down to the street outside. Can you see him? Yūki teased. It looks as though he's gone already, said O-Riki, still lost in thought. So, is he this affliction of yours, then? he pressed her. That's about the size of it… Only no doctor or hot-spring cure can do anything for it. She smiled with faint regret. How I should like to meet him, this beau of yours! What does he look like? Which famous actor would play him? You're in for a surprise, I fear. He's tall and swarthy—a real Fudō.* Ah, so it was his personality, then, that you fell for? He's the sort of man to squander an entire fortune in a house like this. Don't misunderstand me, he was kind and all, but he had no other redeeming qualities whatsoever—he was totally devoid of humour, interest, everything! But then why did you fall for someone like that? asked Yūki, sitting up. I dare say I'm the kind to lose my head... Lately there isn't a night that goes by when I don't see *you* in my dreams. Sometimes I'll dream that you've got married; others, I'll dream that you've suddenly stopped seeing me. More and more, I'm visited by still-unhappier dreams, so much so that I wake up to find my pillow slip drenched in tears. O-Taka falls sound asleep the moment her head hits the pillow, and starts to snore. How I envy her! No matter how weary I am, my mind starts to race the moment I lie down to sleep, and all kinds of thoughts come flooding into my head. It makes me happy to know that you see how these things weigh on me and make an effort to understand, but I doubt that you can really know what it is like for me. At any rate, there's no point in moping. I put on a brave face in front of others, but all that happens is that they think I haven't a care in the world. I even have clients who think I don't know the meaning of hardship. It must be karma. I doubt there's another person in this world as wretched as I am. She wept bitterly

* Also known as Acala ('the Immovable'), Fudō is wrathful deity in the pantheon of East Asian Buddhism.

as she lamented her lot. What a strange and melancholy tale you tell. I want to comfort you, but, without knowing the ins and outs of it, I hardly know how. If you truly have begun to see me in your dreams, you could have told me you wanted us to marry, but you haven't so much as hinted at it! Why ever not? As the ancient proverb has it, no meeting in this life is ever by chance. I wish you'd just come out with it and told me that you loathe your profession so very much. I'd assumed that, for a woman with a temperament such as yours, this floating, wayward life must have suited you. What course of events was it that brought you to this life? I should like to know so very much, if telling it isn't too painful for you. Lately I've found myself wanting to tell you, but tonight I cannot. But why? Oh, don't ask me why. It's selfish of me, I know, but when I've decided to remain silent, nothing can induce me to talk. O-Riki suddenly stood up and went out onto the veranda. The moon shone brightly in the cloudless sky, its cold light bathing the figures whose shadows passed by down below to the echo of *koma-geta*. Yūki-san? What is it? he said, now standing beside her. Sit here, she said, taking his hand. Do you see that little boy over there buying peaches from the fruitmonger? He looks so sweet, don't you think? He's the son of the man who came here earlier. He's not yet four. How is it that the heart of one so young can harbour so much hatred? Whenever he sees me, he cries, Devil! Devil! Am I really so very wicked? As O-Riki gazed up at the sky, she heaved a deep sigh that seemed to ask, How much more of this can I endure?

4.

Somewhere on the outskirts of the new quarter was an alley running between two rows of slum dwellings. So narrow was the passage between them that the eaves of the greengrocer's and the barber's even touched, and it was so cramped there that on rainy days one could scarcely even open an umbrella. Gutter boards were missing all over the place, forcing people to watch their step to avoid gaping holes. There, at the very end of the terrace, beside a rubbish pile, stood a tiny ramshackle house with its wooden doorframe rotting away and its dilapidated rain shutters falling off. The situation of this house, however, unlike the others, allowed it to have two entrances and a little porch at the rear that gave onto a vacant plot of land overgrown with weeds. Along a crudely erected bamboo fence, green perilla and Chinese aster tangled with the stalks of climbing beans. It was here that O-Riki's Genshichi lived. His wife was called O-Hatsu. She would not yet have been thirty then, but poverty had made her gaunt and haggard, adding a good seven years to her appearance, while her teeth were no longer uniformly black, and her eyebrows, no longer shaven, had grown wild, lending her an abject appearance.* Faded as it was by too many launderings, she wore her splash-patterned Narumi *yukata* inside out, fixed tightly in place with a narrow *obi*; the fabric at the knees had

* Beauty standards of the period dictated that women of marriageable age blacken their teeth (see p. 61 note) and shave their eyebrows.

been patched but with stitches so small that they were all but invisible to the naked eye. To earn a little extra money, she did piecework making soles for rattan sandals; it was seasonal labour, begun just before the Festival of the Dead, when the heat was at its fiercest, and so she toiled diligently and perspiringly amid great skeins of rattan that she had slung from the ceilings to save her time. Never once did she take her eyes from her handiwork, seeming to find a sad sort of pleasure in that gradual accumulation of finished soles. Sunset had come and gone, but Takichirō was nowhere to be seen. And where on earth was Genshichi? she wondered, as she tidied away her tools and lit her *kiseru*, blinking her weary eyes. She transferred the embers from under an earthenware teapot to the brazier used for smoking out mosquitoes and carried it over onto the little porch. Then, having collected some sprigs of cedar, she placed them on top of the embers and blew to kindle the fire. Wisps of perfumed smoke began to rise, sending the mosquitoes and their terrible buzzing up into the eaves. It was only then that she heard the clatter of Takichirō's *geta* coming along the boards in the alley. Mama, I'm home! And I've brought Papa with me, too! he cried from the front door. What time do you call this? I was getting worried. I'd begun to think you'd gone off to that temple on the hill. Quickly now, come inside. Takichirō went in first, followed by a worn-out-looking Genshichi. Welcome home, she said. It was so hot today. I thought you'd be back earlier, so I drew a bath for you. The water's still there if you'd like to freshen up. You should have a bath, too, Takichirō. Yes, Mama! the little boy cried and set about untying his *obi*. Wait, just a minute! Let me check the temperature of the water first, said O-Hatsu. Having placed the washbasin in the sink, she filled it with hot water from the kettle, mixed it into the tepid bathwater, and laid out a flannel. There now, just right! Bath the boy as well, would you? You look awfully tired. I hope it isn't heatstroke. Why don't you have a good long soak? You'll be right as rain in no time. I'll have dinner ready for you when you're done. Go on, the boy's waiting. So he is, said Genshichi, as though only just coming to his senses. As he untied his *obi* and lowered himself into the bath, he was assailed by memories of his former self. Never in his wildest dreams would he have imagined back then that, one day, he would find himself taking a bath in a washtub in the kitchen of some hovel—much less that would be spending his days helping labourers on a construction site push a cart around. It was hardly the life that his parents had envisioned for him, either. And all this because of a foolish dream he had once had; the thought weighed on him so onerously that he almost forgot to wash. Wash my back for me, Papa! the boy demanded innocently. You'll get eaten alive by the mosquitoes if you don't hurry up and get out, his wife cautioned. Oh, right… he said, and immediately set about washing Takichirō before seeing to himself. When he eventually stepped out of the bath, his wife handed him a crisp, freshly starched *yukata*. He put it on, wrapped an *obi* about his waist, and sat down to enjoy the cool breeze. Presently, O-Hatsu appeared, carrying an old tray. The lacquer was beginning to peel, and the legs wobbled as she set it down. I've made your favourite, *hiya-yakko*, she said, serving the cold tofu in a little bowl and garnishing it with green perilla leaves, which she heaped on top. Meanwhile, while they were not looking, Takichirō had taken the rice bucket from the table and was dragging it around, shouting, Heave-ho! Heave-ho! Heave-ho! Come here, you little rascal! said Genshichi, tousling the boy's hair with one hand and picking up his chopsticks with the other. He began to eat, but, for some unaccountable reason, the food seemed tasteless and his throat felt swollen. I'm afraid I don't have much of an appetite tonight, he said, setting down his bowl. What do you mean, don't have an appetite? Any other man who did your sort of work could devour three bowls of rice and still be ravenous! Are you ill? Or just too tired to eat? I feel fine. I'm afraid I just don't much feel like eating. That old story, is it? said his wife, a look of hurt in her eye. What is it this time? Did the fare at the Chrysanthemum Well taste better? What good is there thinking about all that now, in your position? Oh, that girl saw you as an easy target from the moment she clapped eyes on you. All you'd need is a bit of money, and she'd be all over you again in the blink of an eye. You can tell at a single glance: it's the business of any girl like that to seduce each and every man who walks by, all with a bit of white face powder and some pretty clothes. Oh! if only you'd open your eyes, you'd see that it's because you're poor now that she's stopped lavishing her attentions on you. All this resentment you still have is but proof of your lingering attachment to the girl. Haven't you heard what became of that young lad from the sake dealer's in the back alley? He fell so hard for O-Kaku over at the Two Leaves that he embezzled and squandered every last yen he collected from customers settling their bills; then, to plug the gap, the young whippersnapper even turned his hand to gambling! Sure enough, he came a cropper, though, and from then on quickly fell into a life of crime. With nowhere to turn, they say he even tried to plunder a storehouse. Apparently, he's in gaol now, eating prison rations, and good old O-Kaku couldn't care less. Oh no, she just sits pretty, going about her business without a care in the world, thriving, even, and never a word of reproach is levelled against her. Such are the perks of her profession. Well, you know what they say: fool you once… There's no point dwelling on it. What you need is to get a grip. Focus all your energy on work and try earning some money. If you were to drop dead tomorrow, the boy and I would be destitute. We'd wind up begging in the streets. If only you'd be a man and earn some money, then it wouldn't be just O-Riki you could afford, but a Komurasaki, an Agemaki!* You could even build a villa to keep her in clover. Wouldn't that be nice? But you can forget all that for the time being. For now, just eat your dinner and content yourself. Look, you've even gone and upset the poor boy! When Genshichi turned to look, he saw that Takichirō had set down his bowl and chopsticks and was looking back and forth from one parent to the other—too young to understand, but

* The names of two of the most renowned courtesans of the Edo period.

looking distressed all the same. The sight of the child pricked Genshichi's conscience. What had he done to deserve this? How was it that he could not escape the devilish allure of that woman, when he had such a sweet child to dote on at home? He had only himself to blame. Oh, what a fool I've been! Please, don't ever mention her name again. Hearing it only reminds me what an almighty mess I've made of things. These days, I just hang my head in shame. How is it that I can still think of the woman who has been the ruin of me? But don't worry—if I can't eat tonight, it's only because I'm so exhausted. Give the boy as much as he likes. With that, Genshichi lay flat out on his back and began to fan himself frantically. It was not the smoke from the mosquito fire that was stifling him, however, but rather the torrid emotions that were smouldering in his breast.

5·

Whoever was it who first dubbed them white devils knew what he was talking about, for there truly was something infernal, something of Avīci itself, about that place.* Even the ones who seemed utterly devoid of guile could so easily drown men in the Pool of Blood or chase debtors up the Mountain of Needles. They lured men in with a mellifluous voice, their call every bit as alluring as a pheasant's before it

* Known in Japanese as *mugen jigoku*, or 'the Hell of Unbounded Suffering', Avīci is the eighth and lowest of Buddhism's so-called Hot Hells.

goes and, with a dreadful squawk, devours the adder that it has caught whole. And yet they, too, were human; they, too, had spent ten lunar months in their mother's womb; they, too, had suckled at their mother's breast and been dandled, playing pat-a-cake on her lap; when given the choice between money and sweet treats, they, too, had reached out their hand for the confection. Sincerity was but a figment of their trade: yet even so, perhaps one girl in a hundred might shed tears of genuine love for a man. You know Tatsu, from the dye-house? one of these girls might say. Well, just yesterday, at Kawada's, he was carrying on again with that O-Roku—you know, the one who never stops talking? I could hardly bear to watch! He dragged her out into the street, and they each started giving the other what for. Really, he'll get nowhere acting up like that. And how old is he now, anyway? Didn't he turn thirty the other year? I keep telling him, what he needs is to settle down and start a family, but he won't hear of it. Every time, he just mutters some half-excuse and pays me no mind whatsoever. His father's getting on in years, you know, and, as for his dear mother, the poor old girl's going blind. He ought to pull himself together, to spare their worries at least. And here I am, ready to wash his livery coat and mend his underdrawers, waiting all the while for the day when that immature sod will make an honest woman of me. The more I think about it, the more I loathe what I do. I've had it up to here! And I'm in no mood to bring in punters... Oh, she was at her wit's end, all right. But while today her tongue bewailed her lover's cruelty, ordinarily it swindled and deceived. Worse yet, now all this thinking had brought on a headache. Ah, it's the sixteenth of the month today! says another girl. The Festival of the Dead... Today the children will all be going to pay their respects to Lord Enma—all dressed up in their best clothes, all with a little pocket money and smiles on their faces. Doubtless, each of them has two respectable parents. My little Yotarō will probably have been given the day off, but no matter where he goes or what he does, he's sure to be jealous of the others. What with a vagrant and a drunkard for a father, and the humiliation of having a mother like me who paints herself to earn a crust... Even if he knew where to find me, he'd never visit. I remember seeing him last year, during the flower-viewing at Mukōjima. There, in all my finery, with my hair done up in a married woman's chignon, I was strolling with some of the other girls, and that's when I spotted him in a teahouse on the riverbank. I called out to him, and he turned around. Can it really be you, Mama? he asked in astonishment, amazed at how youthful I looked—to say nothing of the elaborate hairstyle I wore, adorned as it was with one of those ornamental flower hairpins thought fashionable at the time, its trailing blossoms made of silk fluttering in the breeze. How heartbreaking it must have been for the poor boy to see me flirting and joking with clients. When last we saw each other, he told me he'd been apprenticed to a candlemaker in Komagata. He promised me that he'd brave whatever hardships came his way so that he could be independent and that his father and I might have an easier life. Whatever you do, just hang on till then, Mama, he said to me. Try to make ends meet and lead a respectable life. And above all, please don't remarry, I beg of you! Alas, it's hard for a woman to make a decent living making matchboxes. And I'm too weak to go crawling about some kitchen floor, scrubbing like a maid. So, if there's nothing for it but to work, I'd rather spend my days and nights doing this. At least it isn't so physically taxing. Never once did I dream that this would be the easy way out, although I'm sure that little boy of mine despises me. He probably finds it all tawdry and unmentionable. It's funny, you know: ordinarily, I never give the hairstyle I wear a second thought, but today for some reason it feels especially shameful. As she sat there in front of the mirror at twilight, there were tears in her eyes... The Chrysanthemum Well's O-Riki was no devil incarnate, either. There were circumstances that had carried her to this mire where she now spent her days tempering the most brazen of lies with badinage. For her, words such as love and passion were as flimsy as Yoshino paper,* as fickle as the light of a firefly. In her world, tears were not shed lightly. A man might kill himself over a woman, only for her to say, How sad! and turn the other way. This habit of deflecting grief was well cultivated. Even so, there were times when sorrows and cares would swell in her chest. But, for fear that others might see her cry, she preferred to throw herself on the floor of the *tokonoma* in one of the upstairs rooms and whimper there quietly. She would hide this even from her bosom friends. And so, while the

---

* A traditional Japanese tissue paper.

world thought of her as spirited and resolute, she was secretly as fragile as a spider's thread that might break at the merest touch. It was the evening of the sixteenth day of the seventh lunar month, and all the houses of the pleasure quarter were filled with clients singing popular ballads and serenades. In one of the downstairs rooms of the Chrysanthemum Well, half a dozen shop clerks were gathered. They crooned a very out-of-tune 'The Province of Kii', and then one of them, with a tin ear and a voice of lead (although with alarming confidence!) began to warble, The hills are draped in mist… Why don't you show us what you're made of, O-Riki? one of them eventually said. Yeah, come on, darling, give us a tune! another pressed her. Yielding to their entreaties, she sang the song that had won her renown: I will not speak his name, though he be among us… After much hooting and applause, she carried on: My love is like the log bridge over Hosodani River: I fear to cross it, and yet I must… But then, suddenly, as though having been reminded of something, she stopped. I'm sorry, you'll have to excuse me a moment, she said, setting her *shamisen* down and getting up to leave. Where are you going? You can't just leave us! the men chorused indignantly. Teru! O-Taka! Would you look after them for a little? I'll be right back… With that, she hurried out and down the hall. Then, at the entrance, she quickly slipped on her *geta* and, without so much as a backward glance, vanished into the darkness of the alley opposite.

She ran and ran as fast as she could. If only her legs would have carried her, she would have run far away, as far as China, India, Timbuctoo. How she despised her life! But where would she go? To a place where there were no voices, no noise, just silence, perfect silence! where she could rest without a care in the world. How much longer was she to be trapped in this tedium, in this monotony, in this wretched, miserable, hopeless insanity? Was this any life? Was this really what life was? How she despised it. Lost in her reveries, she stopped and leant against a tree by the side of the road. I fear to cross it, and yet I must… The words of the song haunted her. What choice do I have? she thought. Now I, too, must cross that bridge. My father lost his footing as he tried to make his way across, and they say that his father before him met the same fate. I came into this world saddled with the burden of generations, but I cannot leave it, for there are things I must do yet. Though it shames and saddens me, there is nobody else to think, What a pity it is! And if I told others of my woes, they'd simply brush them aside, insisting that it goes with the territory. Well then, come what may, come what may… No matter how I think about it, I haven't any idea what's to become of me. And in that case, I might as well go on being the Chrysanthemum Well's O-Riki. Am I so heartless? so ungrateful? I mustn't think such things. There's no telling where thoughts like that might lead. What with the life I lead, the work I do, my past, my fate, I'm no ordinary woman, that's for sure. To think otherwise would only entail more pain… What's the matter with me? What am I doing, standing here? Why did I come here? I must be a fool—or mad! I can scarcely even tell myself. I'd best be getting back.

O-Riki left the darkness of the alley and turned on a whim into a bustling street lined with night stalls. The faces of the passers-by seemed so very small, and even those of people who brushed past her seemed oddly distant. It was as if she were floating ten feet above the ground and looking down on them. She could hear the indistinct chatter of their voices, but the sounds echoed as if she had fallen to the bottom of a well. Blocking the voices out, she gave herself over entirely to her own thoughts. She passed by a large crowd of people standing around a man and woman who were arguing heatedly right there in the street, but to her it was as though she were walking through a field on a desolate plain stripped bare by winter. Nothing drew her attention. No scenery caught her eye. Everything faded away as the blood rushed to her head. Feeling disoriented and panicked, she stopped in her tracks, wondering whether she might be losing her mind. Just then, somebody tapped her on the shoulder. And just where do you think you're going, O-Riki?

6.

Come and see me on the sixteenth, she had said. I'll be waiting. But, along with everything else, the promise had slipped her mind entirely, and it was only now, bumping into Yūki Tomonosuke quite by chance, that she recalled having made it. The uncustomary look of bewilderment on her face made him laugh heartily. Indeed, it was curious to see her so flustered. I'm so embarrassed, she said. I'd gone for a wander to clear my head. I was miles away. I'm very glad to see you. How heartless of you to make a promise and then not keep it! he chided her. Think of me what you like, but allow me to explain, won't you? She tugged at his arm and began to lead him through the crowds. We ought to be careful, he said. There's a real horde out tonight. Don't mind them. Come on, this way...

By now, the party in the downstairs room at the Chrysanthemum Well was in full swing. O-Riki's unexpected departure had made the men only rowdier. Back at last, eh, darling? she heard one of them shout as she reached the entrance. Really, that's some way to treat paying customers! If you don't come in here and show us that pretty little face of yours right this minute, you'll be in our bad books for good! Ignoring this show of bravado, O-Riki led Yūki directly upstairs. I'm afraid I have a headache, so I'm in no state to drink with them, she told one of the other girls. Right now, the smell alone of sake would probably be enough to make me drunk and pass out. I'm going to lie down for a little while, and then we'll see. Please convey my humblest apologies to those gentlemen. Are you sure? asked Yūki anxiously. Won't they be angry? What if they kick up a fuss? Won't that cause trouble for you? What, those melon-heads?* What are they going to do? They can get as angry as they like. She ordered a flask of sake from one of the servants and waited

* A pejorative term for shop boys in Higuchi's day, thought to derive from a similarity between the pale flesh of the melon and the sickly pallor of the of the young clerks, who were worked so hard that they rarely saw daylight.

impatiently for it to arrive. I'm afraid I'm not going to be much fun tonight, Yūki-san. I feel rather out of sorts. It's just that I have a few things on my mind, you see. I need a drink. Only, please, don't try to stop me. And if I drink too much, you will look after me, won't you? I've never seen you drunk before. By all means, drink if it will cheer you up. Only, won't it give you another headache? What can have put you in such a foul temper? I wonder. Won't you tell me what it is? he asked. I will, but only after I've had a drink. Promise me that you won't be shocked. With a knowing smile, she took a large tea bowl, filled it with sake, and drained it thrice without pausing for breath.

Ordinarily, she paid little attention to Yūki's appearance, but, curiously enough, that evening, she found him somewhat changed. He was a tall man with an imposing build, and he had a calm and authoritative manner of speaking. His sharp, penetrating gaze was truly a sight to behold. His thick head of hair had been cut short, and only now did she notice the sharp hairline at the nape of his neck. What is it that's caught your eye? he asked. I was just looking at your face, she replied. My face?! he said, glaring at her. How you frighten me when you give me that look! She laughed. Joking aside, he said, there is something different about you tonight, you know. I don't mean to rile you by asking, but has something happened? No, nothing's happened. Nothing out of the ordinary, at least. You already know about the troubles I've been having with that man I mentioned. But none of that worries me. I haven't given him a second thought. No, it's just my fickle nature.

I've only got myself to blame for this miserable state I'm in. Just look at me: a girl of low birth. And you, a gentleman of stature! We have entirely different outlooks. Even if I were to tell you, could you ever understand me? Could you really condescend that low? Who's to say? Laugh at me if you will, but tonight I'm going to reveal everything to you. But where to start? My stomach is in knots, and I can hardly speak... Once again, she drained her cup dry.

There are no two ways about it, you must understand. I'm nothing but a common whore. Surely it will come as no surprise for you to learn that I'm not some pure and innocent young maiden. However prettily it's dressed up—they even call us girls lotus flowers among the mud—if we didn't mire ourselves in sin, tainting ourselves, we'd never get a single client, let alone thrive. You aren't like the other men who visit me. But take a moment to imagine what they're like. There are times when I wonder what it would be like to lead an ordinary life, but feelings of bitterness and shame always follow. Sometimes I think how much better it would be to settle down with a husband even in a tiny hovel in some back alley. But I can never do that. And so instead, whenever a man visits me, I have to conceal my misery and tell him how wonderful and handsome he is, how it's love at first sight. Some of them even believe all that empty flattery and tell me they'd take a wretch like me for a wife. Would that make me happy? Would marrying one of those men be the answer to my prayers? I wonder. But you I liked from the very start—so much that if a single day goes by without my seeing you, I pine for you. But would I be your wife if you asked me? I can't stand the thought of belonging to anyone. But then, nor can I bear it when you're gone. Fickle really is the word for it. And what do you suppose it was that made me this way? Failure upon failure upon failure… Three generations of it! My father made a mess of his life, too, you see… As tears filled her eyes, Yūki bid her to speak more about her family. My father was a craftsman, and my grandfather was a scholar—he could read and write—but they say he went mad. Apparently, I bear a certain likeness to him. He wrote scraps that were of no use to man nor beast, and the government forbade their publication. Unable to reconcile himself to this, they say he starved himself to death. Though of humble origin, he had decided in his sixteenth year to devote himself entirely to a life of study, but in the end he achieved nothing and became a laughing-stock. He died in obscurity, and I heard my father lament this fact repeatedly, ever since I was a child. When he was three years old, my father fell from the porch and lost the use of one leg, because of which he came to loathe being among other people. Consequently, he set up shop as a goldsmith at home, but, owing to his pride and his arrogance, he was not well liked, and nobody patronized him. Ah, how I remember the winter of my seventh year. I can still see the scene now: my parents and I huddled together in our old *yukata*; my father leaning there against the pillar and working diligently at his craft, seemingly oblivious to the bitter cold; my mother tending to a cracked pot on that battered old stove. I was sent out to run an errand. I remember clutching the miso strainer in one hand and some small change so tightly in the other. I ran gaily all the way to the rice merchant's shop, but on the way back, my hands and feet went numb from the cold. Not far from home, I slipped on some ice that was covering one of the gutter boards and went flying, dropping everything I had in my arms. The rice scattered everywhere, falling through the gaps in the boards, and the ground below was covered in mud and filthy water. I just kept staring at it, but there was nothing I could do. I was only a child then, but I knew that my parents had no money. I knew how difficult things were. I couldn't go home empty-handed. I stood there crying for a while. Not a single person stopped to ask me what the matter was. But then, even if they had done, nobody would have bought me any rice. Had there been a river or a pond nearby, I'm sure that I would have resolved to drown myself in it. For all my words, I can scarcely begin to tell you what it was really like. That was when I began to lose my mind. Worried by my long absence, Mother came out to look for me. When we arrived back, nothing was said about what had happened. Neither she nor my father uttered so much as a word of reproach. The house was as silent as a grove at a shrine; now and then I would hear one of them sigh, but that sound was more painful to me than the blow of a sword. I held my breath, trying to make myself invisible, until my father at last said, We'll go without food today...

Her words trailed off. Unable to hold back the tears welling in her eyes, she pressed a red handkerchief to her face and bit down on the edge to stop her sobbing. For a long time neither of them spoke, and the only sound was the buzzing of mosquitoes attracted by the aroma of sake.

When O-Riki looked up at last, her cheeks still bore the trace of tears, but she was smiling wistfully now. That's the kind of poverty I come from—my only inheritance, these occasional bouts of madness... But how tedious this must be for you. Please, forgive me for having foisted all my troubles on you tonight. I won't say another word about them. Shall I call for someone to lighten the mood? she asked. No, do go on, please! Your father, did he die young? Yes, but it was Mother who went first. She was consumptive. Father followed not even a week after she died. He wouldn't even be fifty yet if he were alive today. I'm not just saying this because the man was my father, but he really was a master at his craft, you know. But no matter how fine a craftsman he may have been, there was nothing he could do, being born into a family like ours. I know that only too well myself... Here, her mind seemed to drift off. But you have ambitions in life, don't you? Yūki asked all of a sudden. Ambitions?! said O-Riki, seemingly taken aback by the question. A strainer of rice is all the ambition people like me can afford. No, I'll never see myself travelling in a jewel-encrusted palanquin... You needn't be shy around me. Why, it was obvious the very first day I met you! There's little point in hiding it now: it would be crass even to try. So what if you are ambitious, good grief?! Please, you mustn't embolden me with words like that, she said, slumping back in despondency. I'm just a nobody. Another silence fell.

Darkness, too, had long since fallen. The men in the room downstairs had already gone, and the two of them could hear somebody putting up the rain shutters on the frontage outside. Astonished by the lateness of the hour, Yūki made ready to leave. It was then that O-Riki suggested he spend the night. After all, she said, his *geta* would have been tidied away already, so he was stuck there. Besides, what with the shutters up, he could hardly leave now, slipping out through the gap in the door like some phantom. With no alternative, he accepted her invitation. With one final clattering of the rain shutters, the lamplight from the street was blocked out entirely. Now the only sound remaining was that of footsteps, which belonged a lone policeman making his night rounds under the eaves below.

7·

What good were those memories now? How often had he told himself just to forget her? to give her up? Yet still his thoughts drifted irresistibly back to the past. Only last year, during the Festival of the Dead, they had made matching *yukata* and gone together to pay their respects at the shrine in Kuramae. Despite himself, he was haunted by memories such as these. Ever since the festival had begun this year, he had lacked the energy to go out and work. This will never do! his wife remonstrated. Watch your tongue, woman. And not another word out of you! he said, rolling over. Well, if I didn't say something, we'd never see the day out! If you really are poorly, then take some medicine. As far as I can tell, there's no point seeing a doctor, though. It's something else that ails you… If only you'd cheer up, you'd see there's bugger all wrong with you. Oh, won't you please come to your senses and just knuckle down? How you do go on, woman! If it's cheering up I need, then go out and buy me some sake. That's the best medicine. If only we could afford to buy sake, I wouldn't be trying to force you to go out to work now, would I? I work all hours, from dawn till dusk, but the paltry fifteen *sen* that I earn from it doesn't even begin to cover things! With three mouths to feed, we don't even have enough to drink hot water, and you ask me to buy sake?! What a nerve! The festival's already upon us, and I can't even give the poor boy a paltry rice-flour dumpling to eat. There's no money to make any decorations or offerings for the spirits of the dead. All I've been able to do is to light a single votive candle. And whose fault do you suppose that is?! It's all because you've let yourself be hooked in by that O-Riki! Oh, what a fool you are! It's a terrible thing to say, but you're an irresponsible father and an impious son. Won't you at least spare a thought for the boy's future? Get a grip, man! For heaven's sake! Drink and you'll feel better for an hour or two, but if you don't seriously mend your ways, who knows what's to become of us… Without saying a word, Genshichi just lay there on his back, motionless, staring up at the ceiling; only the occasional deep sigh hinted at the bitterness of his regrets. After all she's done to you, you still can't forget her, can you? After ten years of marriage and even my bearing you a child, she thought, you still put me through such heartache and hardship, you still make our son go about in rags, and you still force us to live in this hovel that's little better than a doghouse, where we're mocked and despised by everyone. Even during the spring and autumn equinoxes, when everybody else in the neighbourhood goes about exchanging *botamochi*, we're shunned because we can't offer any in return—and they think they're doing us a favour! Some favour… Ours is the only house that gets left out. And it's one thing for the man who can escape it all by going out to work—I doubt it weighs on his mind—but for the woman who has to stay at home, trapped here, utterly wretched and miserable… It's only natural that I should feel ashamed and humiliated. How could I not, when each day I see the look in people's eyes as they greet me? But it's fine for you! All you ever do is think about that mistress of yours. How is it that you can love somebody so heartless? Even in your daydreams, you see her and mutter her name, and all the while you leave your wife and son forgotten. Have pity! Do you intend to give your life to her? What a mean, despicable, cruel man you are… Tears of bitterness welled in her eyes, choking her.

Neither of them said a word. The night was drawing in, and in the fading light their little house in that back alley felt somehow even gloomier and more desolate. O-Hatsu lit one of the lamps and then set out the brazier to drive away the mosquitoes. As she stood there, forlorn and gazing out the door, she spotted Takichirō skipping home and carrying what looked like a large parcel in both his hands. Mama!

Mama! Look what I've got! he cried, running up to her with a big smile. It was a *castella* cake from the Sunrise shop in the new quarter. My! Who gave you such a lovely cake? asked O-Hatsu. I hope you thanked them. Yes, I bowed properly, Mama. It was the devil lady from the Chrysanthemum Well. O-Hatsu's face blanched. Oh, that brazen hussy! Hasn't she crucified this family enough? Must she now stoop so low as to manipulate you—a child!—just to tug on your father's heartstrings? This is beyond the pale! What did she say when she gave it to you? I was playing at a busy spot in the high street when she came up to me with this old man and said she'd buy me some cake if I went with them. I said I didn't want any, but she picked me up and took me with them and bought me some. Can I have it now? The child, of course, could not divine his mother's feelings, and just looked up at her face expectantly. You're much too young to understand these things, but that woman is a devil, don't you know? She cast her charm and turned your father into a lazy good-for-nothing. It's because of her that you don't have nice clothes to wear or a proper roof over your head. It's because of her that we've lost everything! How you could even want to eat something that devil woman has given you is beyond me. But she's certainly sunk her teeth into this family all right. She's insatiable! Oh, I can't bear to have that filthy, stale piece of cake in this house. Just looking at it turns my stomach! Throw it away, will you? Throw it away! What are you waiting for? Do you really want it that much? You little fool… She grabbed the gift and threw it into the vacant plot behind the house.

The wrapping paper tore and the cake went tumbling out, rolling through a gap in the wild-grown bamboo fence, and landing in what sounded like the ditch on the other side. O-Hatsu! shouted Genshichi, bolting up all of a sudden. His wife did not even turn around. What do *you* want? she replied, glaring at him out of the corner of her eye. That's it, I've had it up to here with your insolence! Can't you just pipe down for once?! Why all this shouting and abuse? All because somebody gave the boy a piece of cake? He didn't do anything wrong, the poor lad! Stop taking it out on him when it's me you're angry with! Where did you learn these manners anyway? Slandering me to my own son! Some wife you are! And if O-Riki really is a devil, then frankly you must the Queen of Hell! Everyone knows that a whore's heart is fickle, but they never talk about what it is to live with a sullen wife, do they? You think I'm going to stand for that, do you? I may be just a labourer, but whether a man pulls a rickshaw or shovels shit, the head of the family is still the head of the family! I'm tired of keeping such an ungrateful wretch in this house. I want you out! Go! Go wherever you like, but just go! You really are a tedious old bitch! he scolded her. You can't! It would be too cruel! she wailed. And how have I slandered you? I said all those things because the boy doesn't understand, because of O-Riki's scandalous behaviour! How utterly callous of you to twist my words like that and try to turn me out onto the street. It's only because I care about this family that I said it. If I wanted to leave, would I really have endured such penury, such hardship, and for so long?

Well, if it's the penury and hardship that's gnawing at you, you're free to leave at any time. If it weren't for you, at least I wouldn't be such a beggar and the boy would get a moment's peace. I've had enough of your incessant stocktaking of my faults, and I've had enough of your jealousy! I'm sick of hearing about it! If you won't leave, it's all the same to me. You can stay here in this hovel for all I care. I'll take the boy and go myself. Then you can crow all you want! So, what's it to be? he spat at her. Am I leaving, or are you? So, then, you really do mean to divorce me? Work that out all by yourself, did you? This was not the husband O-Hatsu knew. As tears welled in her eyes, feelings of shame mixed with misery and despair. She could scarcely get her words out. It was wrong of me, she said. Please, I'm sorry. I should never have thrown away the cake that O-Riki was kind enough to give us. You're right, of course: maybe I am the real devil in all this. I won't say another word about her. Not another word, ever, I swear! Only, please, reconsider the divorce, I beg of you! You know I don't have any family apart from my uncle, the caretaker, who stood in for the matchmaker and my parents at our wedding. If you divorced me, I don't know where I'd go. Please, forgive me, I beg you! Even if you despise me, let me stay for the boy's sake. I'm sorry! she wailed, her hands placed on the ground in supplication. No, on no account! said her husband. I want you gone. As a stony silence set in, he turned to face the wall, indicating that he had no intention of listening to another word of O-Hatsu's. He never used to be this cruel, this hateful, O-Hatsu thought. Is this what happens when another woman steals a man's heart? Of course, she would be left to her tears, but would he also eventually abandon his precious son, letting him starve to death? The time for apologies, she knew, had passed. Takichirō! Takichirō! she cried out, summoning the boy. Who do you like better, your father or me? I hate Papa, he never buys me anything, the child answered innocently. So you'd rather stay with Mama, no matter where she goes? Yes, Mama, he replied automatically. Do you hear that? The boy says he wants to stay with me. I'm sure you'll want to keep him because he's your son, but I won't let you. He's coming with me wherever I go. Do you hear me? He's mine! Suit yourself, he said, still lying there with his back to O-Hatsu. I don't need the child or anything else from you. Take him with you wherever you like! I don't need the house or the furniture, either, for that matter. Do what you will with them. What are you on about? You don't have a house or any furniture to give away! From now on, you'll have only yourself to think of. Now you can indulge in all those terrible things that make you so happy. But don't ever come back looking for the boy. I'll never let you have him! Her words were emphatic. She then rummaged around in the wardrobe and took out a small *furoshiki*. I'm taking the boy's nightclothes, his coat, his bib and his sash. It wasn't drink that made you say all this, so I don't expect you'll change your mind in the morning. But still, think carefully about what you're doing. No matter how abject the poverty, they say a child raised by both parents has all the advantages of a rich one. If you leave, he'll be left with only one. Whichever way you look at it, it's the boy who'll suffer. You do realize that, don't you? Oh, only a rotten scoundrel could forgo the love of a child just like that. I suppose this is farewell, then! With that, O-Hatsu picked up the *furoshiki* and stepped out into the street. Go! Clear off! shouted Genshichi, making no effort to stop them…

8.

A few days after the Festival of the Dead had ended, but while the lonesome, pale lights of the paper lanterns still shone, two coffins were borne out of the new quarter. One was taken on its journey by palanquin, whereas the other was slung over men's shoulders, like luggage. The former had set off from the Chrysanthemum Well quietly and with discretion, but still onlookers on the main thoroughfare were wont to whisper. What awful luck that poor kid had falling in love with a worthless layabout like that, one said. And for it to end so tragically for her, too! No, replied another, I heard that they planned it together. There's a witness who spotted the pair of them deep in conversation up at the temple on the hill on the evening when it happened. Maybe she felt duty-bound, if the lad had really fallen so deeply in love with her, suggested a third. Her? Duty? Don't make laugh! What would a common whore know about duty? She probably met him on her way back from the bathhouse. I'll bet he followed her, and she couldn't shake him off. They probably walked side by side, chatting together. But then, I did hear that she was slashed cleanly across the back. The sword grazed her cheek and left a deep gash on the nape of her neck. Faced with all that and more, surely she must have tried to escape. I'll bet that's when he finished her off. But as for him… what a suicide! I never thought much of the man back when he sold bedding, but apparently this was glorious, a proper *seppuku*! They say he looked magnificent. What a loss, at any rate, for the Chrysanthemum Well. A girl like that must have brought in a lot of business. They'll be sorry to lose the clientele, I'm sure… Now in grief, now in jest, each gave voice to his thoughts on the incident. There were all manner of conflicting theories and rumours, but nothing that proved conclusive. One thing was certain, though: bitterness endures, it outlives even death itself. Some did say, after all, that at times a streak of light could be seen over the temple on the hill, wandering there like a lost or vengeful soul.

THIS MORTAL COIL

(Utsusemi)

1.

THE HOUSE HAD a modest five rooms, including the rather small vestibule, but the windows facing north and south allowed a pleasant through-draught, lending the place an altogether airy quality. The gardens, by contrast, were extensive, grown lush with plants and shrubbery and groves of budding trees, making it seem the ideal summer residence. The location, moreover, close to the Koishikawa Botanical Gardens, was blissfully quiet; and so, despite one or two minor inconveniences, it was, in all other respects, a flawless rental property. A little over three months had passed since the 'for rent' sign was posted on the gate, but no tenants had been found yet; and the thread-like branches of the willow that stood by the desolate gate just swayed there forlornly in the wind. The house was beautifully kept, which augured well, so much that every day, without fail, one could be sure that two or three people would come and ask to view it. When they learnt that the deposit was three months' rent, however, and that the monthly rent—payable by the thirtieth of each month—was seven yen and fifty *sen*, they would all, without fail, say, Those are Shitamachi prices, and never come back.* Eventually, though, a man showed up early one morning; he must have been around forty and had on a slightly faded machine-spun *yukata.* Somewhat flustered, he came rushing over to the caretaker, asking to see the house. He was shown around—the caretaker spared no efforts in pointing out this or that feature, apprising him even of the number of cabinets and cupboards in the property—but the man paid no attention to any of this; rather, he appeared to have been quite simply enchanted by the peacefulness of the place and all the fresh air. I'll take it, he said, starting today, if it can be arranged. If I put down the deposit now, we can move in this evening. I do appreciate that it's short notice, but would it be an imposition to have it cleaned right away? There being no objection to this, an agreement was duly reached. When the caretaker enquired what the man did for a living, he received the exceedingly vague answer: Nothing all that special, really. He then asked how many of them would be living there. How many? the man echoed. Four or five, perhaps. But occasionally as many as seven or eight. People come and go. You know how it is. I wouldn't care to be too precise about it. The caretaker thought it all very queer, but that same evening, at dusk, when the cleaning was done, the new tenants moved in. They arrived discreetly, by rickshaw,

* The Shitamachi is Tokyo's 'downtown' area and traditionally more impoverished compared to its rival, the more affluent Yamanote, where the villa is located. The comment here suggests a certain snobbism and wariness of the cheap price, perhaps implying that the prospective tenants would not even deign to rent from Shitamachi people.

the canopy obscuring all view of them. The conveyance glided in through the open gate and set its fares down by the main entrance, where two people alighted and vanished so quickly into the house that nobody had even the chance to make them out. The first of these was a quick-witted woman of around thirty, dressed in the trappings of a maid, while her companion was a frail-looking beauty, not yet nineteen, with hardly a trace of colour in her face or limbs. Her skin was so deathly pale that it almost looked transparent. The caretaker, who arrived shortly after to help, peered at the young woman, incredulous that she could be the wife or sister of the man who had come rushing up to him earlier that day.

The only luggage they had brought with them arrived on a single cart, and once the older of the two women had finished handing out the customary gifts to their new neighbours, the house was plunged once again into an eerie silence; there was none of the usual bustle and excitement of people moving in. In addition to the two women, there was also the man from that morning and, with him, an enormous woman who looked like a cook; as the night wore on, however, yet another rickshaw came tearing in through the gate, bringing with it two more people, one of whom was a refined-looking man of around sixty, his head shaved like a bonze, and the other, a woman with her hair done up in a small bun—his wife, judging by their similar age. The sickly young woman had been put to bed in the innermost room the moment she arrived, her head set to rest upon a pillow stuffed with buckwheat chaff; but, even so, the old couple stayed by her bedside all night long. Though wrought with anxiety, their faces bore a vague resemblance to that of the sleeping girl. Could these have been her parents? Not only the maid and the cook but also the young man referred to the two of them as the mistress and the master, and whenever either of them called for the young man, they simply used his given name, Takichi—and yet, how odd! his was the name on the new nameplate outside.

The very next morning, while the breeze was still cool, yet another man arrived by rickshaw. He had on an unlined woven-silk kimono, fixed in place by an *obi* of white silk crêpe. With a hint of a moustache below his nose, this portly, handsome-looking man appeared to be in his thirties. When he spotted the little nameplate that read KITAMURA TAKICHI, he cried out, This is it! We're here! and alighted from the rickshaw. The cook, seeing all this, removed her *tasuki* and called out, Well! if it isn't the young master from Banchō!* Hearing these words, Takichi went dashing out. You've made it here in record time, sir! We weren't expecting you so early. Seeing as we left you in Ōtsuka only yesterday and all. I'm afraid it couldn't be helped, though. She kept saying that she couldn't bear it there and wanted to go somewhere—anywhere!—else. She just wouldn't listen, sir. Eventually I found this place. Would you care to take a look around? If you'll follow me, sir. The gardens are

* An upmarket area of Tokyo, traditionally associated with prominent *hatamoto* families under the Shogunate, and noblemen during the Meiji era.

extensive, so it's secluded enough, and it isn't overlooked. I believe it makes for quite a lovely spot… Yes, sir, she slept well last night, but I'm afraid she seems to have taken a turn again this morning. Well, why don't you come and see for yourself, sir? he said, leading the way. The portly man followed him into the back room, twirling his moustache anxiously.

2.

On exceedingly good days, she might rest her head in her mother's or father's lap and fall asleep like a little girl, or else devote herself entirely to the cutting-out of paper dolls. If you asked her a question—any question—she would just smile sweetly and pliantly and repeat, Oh, yes! devoid of all meaning. But all it would take was a gust of wind to rustle the trees, and she would grow unsettled, disturbed, and beg everyone—her father, mother and brother included—to let her be, whereupon she would hide herself away and start to sob. That alone would have been one thing, but then there was all her keening and howling. It was my fault! she would shriek in agony, as though her innards were being wrung. Forgive me! Please, forgive me! she kept repeating, staring all the while at an empty point in space in front of her, as if somebody were standing there. But then, there was also many a time when, no sooner would she cease all this than, seizing her opportunity when the day nurse went on her break, she would go dashing out of the room, shouting, I'm coming, I'm coming! You go on ahead! We'll soon be reunited! And so a lid had to be placed on the well, and care was taken to ensure that no sharp objects—a pair of scissors, for instance—were ever left in sight. The risk may well have stemmed from her condition, but at any rate it was nigh on impossible to hold this delicate, lone creature back, and whenever she did take a notion to go running out of the room, even two hulking great men would have found it a challenge to restrain her.

Their family home was in the Banchō area—San-Banchō to be precise—and anybody who passed by and saw the nameplate at the gate would nod knowingly and say, Ah, so that's *their* house, is it? Yet a name of renown can be a double-edged sword. Fearing that it might mar their reputation, the girl's elderly parents had refused to hospitalize her when she fell ill, leasing instead a house under the name of their manservant Takichi and summoning a discreet doctor whom they knew and trusted. As she convalesced, she was left to her own devices, but, having spent a whole month in the same surroundings, she had grown jaded by the lack of diversion and had come to loathe the place. Gradually now, her condition seemed to worsen, to the point where she began to frighten those around her.

While the head of the family was now the son-in-law, whom they had adopted,* this girl remained the only child with any

* In Japan, prominent families with no male heir would traditionally adopt a man as a husband for an unmarried daughter as a means of continuing the family line and name. The implication here is that Masao, the portly 'young master from Banchō', has been adopted and betrothed to Yukiko, hence his twin designation as brother and fiancé.

true ties to the family, and so her parents' grief was immense. The first signs of her malady had revealed themselves that spring, just as the cherry trees were blossoming, and, ever since then, day and night, every moment of her parents' lives had been consumed with worries and cares, ageing them terribly. Each time they would watch on helplessly as their daughter succumbed to one of her attacks, crying out, I won't go back! before running out of the room—then all they could do was to call for Takichi and send him after her. Truly, it was a pitiful sight.

The girl had slept soundly all throughout the previous night, and that morning she woke up before anyone else. She brushed her freshly washed hair and chose for herself a kimono that she liked. Putting it on, she neatly, without any help, tied the *yūzen*-dyed *obi* with a crimson over-sash, making herself instantly so beautiful that nobody would have suspected for an instant that she was unwell. When her parents saw her, they were moved to tears. Her maid brought her a bowl of congee and asked whether she was feeling hungry, but the girl simply shook her head before collapsing into her mother's lap. As she lay there, she asked, Is today the last day of my apprenticeship? Can I go home now? To which her mother said, Whatever are you talking about, child? The last day of your apprenticeship? Go home? Really! Is this not your home? Besides, you haven't anywhere else to go, have you? You mustn't go saying such odd things. But, Mother, I *do* have somewhere to go. Look! there's the rickshaw coming to collect me! When she looked where her daughter was pointing, the girl's mother saw only a large spider's web beneath the holly-wood eaves, glittering there like gold in the morning sun.

Unable to bear it any longer, the mother turned to her husband and whispered in horror and exasperation, Well? Did you hear what she just said? All of a sudden, the wilted look on their daughter's face vanished, and she seemed to liven up. Do you remember the cherry-blossom viewing the other year? she said. What's that, dear? her mother asked. How lovely the school gardens looked! she continued, laughing gaily. You gave me a flower, which I pressed between the pages of a book. I still have it, you know. It was such a pretty flower, but now it's faded. I haven't seen you since then. Why do you no longer come to see me? Why won't you come back to me? Am I never to see you again in this lifetime? It was my fault. It was my fault, I know. But my fiancé, my fiancé, you see, he… Oh, I'm so awfully sorry. It was all my fault. Forgive me! You must forgive me… Suddenly, she wrapped her arms around her chest and writhed as though in agony. Yukiko, you mustn't think idle thoughts! This is your illness talking… There's no school, nor any flowers—and your brother isn't here, either. Why, you're hallucinating, child. If only you'd compose yourself a little, you'd settle down and be your old self again in no time, wouldn't you? There, there. That's better… As her mother rubbed her back, Yukiko lay there, sobbing quietly.

3.

Yukiko! the girl's mother called out when she heard that the young master had arrived. Your brother's come to visit you. But the girl did not so much as turn her head. Ordinarily, she would have been reprimanded for such impudence, but the young master forestalled any chastisement. Oh, it's all right. I don't want to disturb her. Let her be. He took the leather cushion that his adoptive mother proffered him and withdrew from the girl's bedside. Then, turning to the old man, who was sitting silently by a pillar with the breeze on his back, he exchanged a few discreet remarks.

The young master was a man of few words. Every now and then, he would punctuate his speech by fanning himself with an *uchiwa*, as though having only just remembered something, or else tapping the ash from his cigarette before lighting it again and replacing it in his mouth. He would do this, glancing all the while at Yukiko out of the corner of his eye. That poor child, he thought. If only I'd known things would turn out this way, I might have been able to do something. But it's too late now; the horse has bolted. What a pity about Uemura... He bowed his head and sighed. When all's said and done, how little we understand people, the father lamented. My mother was just like this, too, and in the end there was nothing we could do. It's all because the girl's so sheltered, of course; but then again, Uemura was no different. The two of us are too ashamed even to look you in the eye. Only, please, have pity on poor Yukiko. Even in her state, all she does is think of her obligations to you. And she comes out with such heart-wrenching things. It's mortifying to think that she should have lost her mind. And all because we tried to educate her! It could so easily bring shame on the family. Please, try to understand, have some pity for all that I've tried to do to preserve our honour. She may not be bright, but ever since she was little she's never set a foot wrong. It saddens me to think about it now. I know people will call me a foolish old man, but I just can't bring myself to give up and say that she'd be better off dead if she can't get better. She's been saying such strange and terrible things lately that I've worried that the hour of her death might be upon her. She kept saying that Death was coming for her at the house in Ōtsuka, so her mother even summoned this idiot of a fortune-teller, who apparently said that for the next month her life would be in grave danger, or some such rubbish. Such an absurd story, of course, but she just wouldn't let it go. She kept going on and on about that house, so in the end I thought it mightn't be such a bad idea moving. That's when we found this place and came here. No, I doubt she's long for this world. She cries out, I'm dying, I'm dying, almost daily. As you can see, her face has that deathly pallor already. And she hasn't eaten a single bite this week. I tell her time and again that she'll wear herself out if she keeps that up, but it's her condition, you see—she just won't listen to anybody. I'm at my wit's end. Doctor Yasuda came and said that, if we keep leaving it to amateurs and quacks like that, her ravings will only get worse. Each time he asks whether we'll consent to having her admitted to a hospital, but, for all his pressing the idea, her mother is most against it, and so we keep dragging our heels. Of course, a hospital would be much more restrictive than home, but lately she's taken to running off so much. I can't stop her, needless to say, but then neither can Takichi or O-Kura—even the two of them haven't the strength. Naturally, we've covered up the well to prevent her from jumping in, but if she were to get out into the street, we'd find ourselves in a real quandary. When I think about it, I sometimes wonder whether I should just have her admitted, but then I think how sorry she looks and I can never make up my mind. I'm at such a loss. If you have any thoughts of your own, you will tell me, won't you? he said, scratching his shaven head, with a look of vacillation. The young master, who had been nodding along as he listened to the old man's monologue, had nothing to say. The two men merely sighed.

Even without any additional strain, Yukiko's body was weak and easily exhausted, but now, after all those tears earlier, she had collapsed in her mother's lap and fallen asleep. Having summoned the nurse, O-Kura, the girl's mother instructed that she help her put the girl to bed. As they laid her out on the silken futon, she was lost entirely to a world of dreams. The young master got down on his knees and quietly drew nearer to her bedside, where he beheld her profusion of black hair, which had been tied up in a series of folds, resembling what is known as the gingko-leaf style, but one that had been done rather haphazardly and was, by now, altogether dishevelled; her two emaciated, ghostly pale arms, which were stretched out, resting one on top of the other upon the pillow; her *yukata*, which lay open, exposing a glimpse of her breast; and her crimson over-sash, which had come undone and threatened to fall open at any moment. The sight of her was more tragic than it was seductive.

There was a desk beside her pillow. Every now and then, she would call, urgently, for the inkstone to be brought, or say that she wanted to read, in imitation of her schooldays, and they would let her draw to her heart's content. The young master went over to this desk, absentmindedly picked up some sheets of paper that were stacked there and, leafing through them, saw that they were covered in strange-looking characters whose meaning was impossible to discern. Surmising with regret this was Yukiko's hand, he managed to decipher the characters *mura* and *rō*: Ah! he thought, Uemura Rokurō. Uemura Rokurō… Unable to bring himself to read on, he laid the sheet of paper back down on the desk without a word.

4.

The young master said that he had nothing else to occupy him, so he spent the entire day by Yukiko's bedside, stirring only when the nurse would bring ice to cool the girl's head. Won't you let me do it? he said, reaching out his rough hands. No, you mustn't, sir. You'll get your lovely kimono all wet, she said. It's fine, really, just let me try, he replied, opening the cap of the ice bag and clumsily squeezing out the water. Yukiko! Do you know what's happening? Masao's just going to cool your head for you, her mother said, leaning over the young master. But the girl seemed entirely unaware of her surroundings, taking in nothing that was said to her. Her eyes were open, but they just stared up into space. Look! What a beautiful butterfly, she began to say, but then suddenly, in a strangled voice she cried out, No! No, brother, you mustn't! Don't kill it! What's that, Yukiko? I can't see any butterfly. It's just me, I'm right here. Don't worry, I'm not going to kill anything. Now, then. Is that better? Can you see me? Hmm? Can you see me? It's me, your brother, Masao! Won't you pull yourself together! Compose yourself! You're worrying Mother and Father. Now you listen to me, try to understand a little. Ever since you became unwell, they haven't a single decent night's sleep. They're worn out, haggard, and yet still they take care of you with every ounce of strength they have. You have a duty to them as a daughter! How is it that you cannot see this? You used to be such a reasonable girl. Calm yourself and think it through. There's nothing that can be done for Uemura now. If only you'd mourn for him properly and go to offer flowers and incense, he'd be able to rest in peace, as he said in that note, wouldn't he? He severed all ties with this world properly, and with you, too, so he cannot have had any lingering attachments.* Can't you see that by upsetting yourself like this, you're causing your parents so much grief? You may have been unfeeling, but he certainly

* In Buddhism, lingering attachment to worldly cares are a cause of suffering in the afterlife.

didn't resent you for it. He was a reasonable man. Surely you must see that. You said he was the best thing about that school, and how he was always praising you. There's no way that a man like that would go to his death harbouring a grudge against you. His anger was directed at society, everybody knows that; he said as much in that note he left behind. Think about it and come to your senses. If you do, I'll let you do as you want from now on. Think about your poor parents! Just imagine how they're suffering. Enough with all this! Come now. Yes? If you truly want to, you can get better. Today, even. You don't need a doctor or medicine. You just have to make up your mind. Come, will you do that? For me? Come on, Yukiko. Be a good girl. Come on… The girl simply nodded and said, Yes, yes.

At some point, the maids had slipped off, leaving only the girl's father, mother and Masao with her. It was impossible to know whether she had understood any of what had just been said to her, but, in a feeble voice, she called out, Brother! Brother! Masao set the ice bag down and drew nearer. What is it? What's the matter? he asked. Wake me up, she said. My body hurts. She was forever getting excited and running out, only to be caught by one of the men, whereupon she would struggle and thrash about with such terrifying strength as she tried to escape that it was little wonder her body ached and there were cuts and bruises all over her. Yet, even so, her parents could not help finding a glimmer of hope in the fact that she realized this. Do you know who it is that's holding you, Yukiko? the girl's mother asked. It's my brother! she replied without hesitation. If you know that, that's already quite enough, child. And do you understand what he told you just now? Yes! He said the flowers are in full bloom, she said unexpectedly again. The girl's parents and Masao all looked at one another and sighed.

Soon enough, Yukiko's breathing grew laboured. Please, I beg of you, she said in a quiet, halting voice, you mustn't say that. There's nothing I can say in return. What are you talking about? her mother said, looking up. Oh, Uemura-san! Uemura-san, where are you going? Suddenly, she bolted up, brushed aside an astonished-looking Masao's legs and made a run for the veranda. Cries of alarm issued from the kitchen, and Takichi and O-Kura came dashing out. But Yukiko did not get far: she reached the pillar at the end of the veranda and collapsed there. Forgive me! she cried out. It's all my fault! Right from the start, it was all my fault. You did nothing wrong. I… I should have said something. I should have told you about Masao… The girl broke down in tears, and, although she carried on raving, her sobbing made it difficult to understand her broken words. Above her, hanging from the eaves, a half-lowered rattan screen rattled in the wind, only adding to the desolation of this twilight scene.

5.

Yukiko's deliriums were forever the same; for days, weeks, months and more, the words she pronounced were never changing, never tiring upon her lips—Uemura's name, pleas for forgiveness, her mentions of school and letters, her guilt, her promises to follow him, her endearments. And though she may have been present in body, yet her spirit had departed—like a cicada that has cast off its shell. She seemed no longer to comprehend what people said to her. She would now laugh gaily as she dreamt of an innocent past, and now clutch her chest, groaning in torment, unable to escape the anguish that assailed her as the reality of her present returned to her once again.

How pitiful it all was, and how heartrending! Takichi said as much, and O-Kura agreed. Even the heartless cook never once dared to suggest that the young mistress might be to blame for what had happened. I can still see her going off to school now, as if it were yesterday, O-Kura said, wearing her schoolgirl's long-sleeved yellow *haori*, her hair done up in that lovely high chignon, adorned with a white-and-cherry-coloured decoration and held in place with a simple silver hairpin. When, oh when, will she return to her former self? I always thought that Uemura was such a nice man, too… What?! That swarthy bumpkin of a man? I don't care how clever he was—if you ask me, he was never good enough for the young miss. I always thought so, the cook said emphatically. It's pure ignorance that makes you say such nasty things! If you'd spent even three days with the man, you'd understand. Anyone would have followed him to the River Sanzu.* I don't mean to put the young master down when

* In Japanese Buddhism, an equivalent to the River Styx.

I say it, but his nature is so different from that of the other gentleman; it's hard to put into words what a lovely man he was. When I heard about what he'd gone and done, I felt so sad that I shed a tear. But how much more painful it must be for the young mistress. For anyone as scatterbrained as you or me, it may not be such a misfortune, but for a girl as quiet and reserved as she, it must have come as a dreadful blow. It feels wrong to say this about that kind and gentle man, but if it hadn't been for the young master, I doubt she'd be in the terrible state she's in now. Then again, if it weren't for Uemura, everything would have turned out just fine, too. Ah! how much sorrow there is in this world of cares. And all because of the things we do not dare to speak, said O-Kura, grief-stricken by the vicissitudes of life.

Masao's work prevented his coming to visit every day, but still, he would come every other evening, and, alighting from the rickshaw by the willow, he would pass under it and through the gate. Sometimes Yukiko would be glad to see him, and sometimes she would cry and refuse to see him. There were also times when, like an infant, she would just lay her head in Masao's lap and fall asleep. No matter who brought her food, she was stubborn and would refuse even to pick up her chopsticks, but when Masao scolded her for this, she could sometimes be induced to take a little congee from the bowl. Are you feeling better? he would ask. Yes, better. You must get better today. Yes, today I'll get better. I'll get better and I'll make you a *hakama*. I'll sew you a kimono, too. Why, that's very kind of you to offer. You'd better get well soon, then, so that you can get to work. If I do, will you call for Uemura? Will you let me see him? Mmm, yes, of course I'll let you see him. I'll send for him. So you'd better get well soon and not let your parents worry, yes? Yes, I'll be better tomorrow, she said unhesitatingly.

Deep down, Masao knew that he could hardly credit her words, and yet still, the very next day, scarcely able to wait for dusk, he went tearing there in a rickshaw, only to find an entirely different girl from the one he had encountered on the previous evening. Whatever he said, she would flatly say no and refuse even to look at him. She would not allow her parents or Masao or even the servants to come near her. I don't know, she cried, I don't know, I just don't know! The spectacle of this wretched girl, alone in a vast wilderness and surrounded by despair without end, was enough to bring tears to the eye.

Around the middle of the eighth month, when the summer heat suddenly turned fierce, Yukiko's wild outbursts intensified. No longer could she distinguish between people and the objects around her, and her cries now resounded day and night without cease. As sleep deserted her, her eyes grew sunken and her cheeks hollowed, imparting to her a grim, otherworldly appearance. While the nurses were wearied by their exertions, Yukiko's body began to wither. She spoke of having seen Uemura yesterday, and of seeing him again today. And she told of how she could see his silhouette outlined on the opposing bank of the river, standing there in the mist, yet all he would say was, Tomorrow, tomorrow...

Would there ever come a day when she would return to her senses and cry out, Mother! Father! as though waking from a dream? It was in the vague, uneasy hope of seeing this that her parents carried on living from one day to the next. Even to gaze upon this mortal coil brings comfort, as the old line has it.* And yet, how sorrowful the rustling of the willow in the autumn winds…

---

* The opening line from a *waka* poem—specifically, a lamentation—by the monk Shōen (*Kokinshū* 831). The 'mortal coil' mentioned here is the cicada's discarded shell.

Glossary of Japanese Terms

anpan	A sweetened bread roll filled with adzuki-bean paste
awamori	A distilled spirit originally from Okinawa
botamochi	Known in English as peony cakes, these confections are made of glutinous rice and adzuki-bean paste
castella	A variety of cake based on those brought to Japan by the Portuguese in the sixteenth century
chawanmushi	A savoury steamed-egg custard, typically containing chicken, prawn, shiitake mushrooms or fishcake
dango	A kind of dumpling made from rice flour, often served on skewers
furoshiki	A length of cloth used to wrap items
geta	A traditional kind of Japanese footwear resembling a sandal raised on blocks; *koma-geta* are a tall, lacquered variety of these, associated with high-ranking courtesans such as *oiran*
haori	Resembling a loose-fitting jacket, a traditional garment worn over a kimono
kabayaki	A dish of fish or eel, butterflied, marinated and grilled on skewers over charcoal

kiseru	A long pipe used for smoking tobacco
mikoshi	In Shintoism, a portable shrine that serves as a vehicle in which to transport a deity during a festival
obi	A sash tied about the waist
rin	One tenth of a *sen*, or one thousandth of a yen
ryō	A unit of gold, used as currency in the pre-Restoration days
sembei	A kind of rice cracker
sen	One hundredth of a yen
seppuku	Suicide by ritual disembowelment
shamisen	A three-stringed, banjo-like traditional instrument, often used in parlour entertainment
shimada	Popularized in the Edo period, a traditional Japanese hairstyle commonly worn by girls in their late teenage years
shōji	A kind of sliding paper screen
tabi	A traditional split-toe sock
tasuki	A thin sash or cord tied about the back and shoulders to hold up the sleeves of a kimono (often while working)
tatami	Mats made of woven rush, used as flooring in traditional Japanese rooms; also used as a unit of measurement for indoor space
tokonoma	A recessed space or alcove in a traditional Japanese room, used for displaying items such as hanging scrolls, flower arrangements and other decorative objects

uchiwa A typically round, non-foldable fan attached to a fixed handle

yakitori Skewers of grilled chicken

yukata A light, unlined cotton kimono, typically worn in summer

AVAILABLE AND COMING SOON FROM PUSHKIN PRESS CLASSICS

The Pushkin Press Classics list brings you timeless storytelling by icons of literature. These titles represent the best of fiction and non-fiction, hand-picked from around the globe – from Russia to Japan, France to the Americas – boasting fresh selections, new translations and stylishly designed covers. Featuring some of the most widely acclaimed authors from across the ages, as well as compelling contemporary writers, these are the world's best stories – to be read and read again.

THE BOOK OF PARADISE
ITZIK MANGER

THE ALLURE OF CHANEL
PAUL MORAND

SWANN IN LOVE
MARCEL PROUST

THE EVENINGS
GERARD REVE